Abigail's eyes fluttered open. "What... what happened?"

Shaun's heart started beating again.

"Someone broke in." He pulled off his dress shirt, wondering if his voice sounded normal.

"Who? Did you get the computer? Why are you undressing?"

"No. They have it. And I'm taking off my T-shirt to clean your face."

"Oh…" Coughing more vigorously, she tried to sit up, but he pushed her back down before pulling his shirt over his head. "Who's they?"

"I don't know. Do you always ask this many questions?" He didn't intend to answer so sharply, but he was still getting his equilibrium back at almost getting them both killed.

"No, I just… Sorry," she muttered.

He stopped and looked into her eyes. "No, Abigail, I'm the one who's sorry. I almost got you killed for the second time today."

Her eyes filled with tears. "I don't really see it that way, you know. I think you just saved my life for the second time."

KAY THOMAS

BULLETPROOF HEARTS

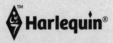

TORONTO NEW YORK LONDON
AMSTERDAM PARIS SYDNEY HAMBURG
STOCKHOLM ATHENS TOKYO MILAN MADRID
PRAGUE WARSAW BUDAPEST AUCKLAND

For Tom, for everything.

Recycling programs
for this product may
not exist in your area.

ISBN-13: 978-0-373-69541-6

BULLETPROOF HEARTS

ABOUT THE AUTHOR

Having grown up in the heart of the Mississippi Delta, Kay Thomas considers herself a "recovering" Southern belle. She attended Vanderbilt and graduated from Mississippi State University with a degree in educational psychology and an emphasis in English. Along the way to publication, she taught high school, worked in an advertising specialty agency and had a very brief stint in a lingerie store.

Kay met her husband in Dallas when they sat next to each other in a restaurant. Seven weeks later they were engaged. Twenty years later she claims the moral of that story is "When in Texas look the guy over before you sit next to him, because you may be eating dinner with him the rest of your life!" Today she still lives in Dallas with her Texan, their two children and a shockingly spoiled Boston terrier named Jack.

Kay is thrilled to be writing for Harlequin Intrigue and would love to hear from her readers. Visit her at her website, www.kaythomas.net, or drop her a line at P.O. Box 837321, Richardson, TX 75083.

Books by Kay Thomas

HARLEQUIN INTRIGUE
1112—BETTER THAN BULLETPROOF
1130—BULLETPROOF TEXAS
1197—BULLETPROOF BODYGUARD
1274—BULLETPROOF HEARTS

CAST OF CHARACTERS

Abigail Trevor—A professor of Southern literature attending her brother's funeral in Washington, D.C. When Abby finds out her brother's hit-and-run accident was murder, she is forced to trust a mysterious stranger to ensure her own safety.

Shaun Logan—Raised in Ireland, Shaun now works in the U.S. as a contract bodyguard security specialist for Zip Technologies. His job is to keep Abby safe, but can he do that and discover who really killed her brother?

Jason Trevor—Abby's brother and the creator of Zip-Net, a completely secure internet wireless protocol. Was he killed for it?

Michael Donner—CEO and founder of Zip Technologies, also Shaun's boss. Famous in the business world for his philanthropy and business sense, Michael is about to sign the deal of a lifetime if Shaun and Abby can find the answers he needs.

Karen Weathers—Abby's mentor and friend currently living in a Dallas rehab facility due to a stroke. Will she be used as a pawn while Abby and Shaun look for clues?

Harlan Jeffries—Shaun's best friend from Iraq. Can Harlan help Shaun keep Abby safe?

Hodges—Reports to Michael Donner. Shaun has worked with him before at Zip Technologies.

Chapter One

Day One—Morning

Watching the strangers scurry past her brother's grave, Abby Trevor felt blessedly numb everywhere...except her feet. The designer shoes she'd bought on a whim last spring with Jason hurt like crazy and pain was the only thing keeping her focused. The pinch in her right instep reminded her of the day she and her brother had shopped themselves silly in New York. At the moment that needle-like sensation was the way she knew the coffin in front of her was not some hideous nightmare as the rain fell in sheets from the dark morning sky.

If she let herself believe for one second the sea of black umbrellas around her was a dream, she'd stand up, kick off those wretched shoes and run screaming from the drowning cemetery. That would certainly set the tongues to wagging, especially here in Washington, D.C.

But she wouldn't disgrace her brother or his memory that way. Her mama's Southern belle training was too ingrained in her, despite the fact that she was one thousand miles from the Mississippi Delta and the small town that had been the cradle of her genteel upbringing.

Still, that home training—and her uncomfortable shoes—kept Abby's butt firmly planted in the soggy funeral home seat under the green awning. She'd never be able to stand the sight or scent of stargazer lilies again. Thunder rumbled in the distance, serving as another reminder that despite the surreal atmosphere, this was no dream.

Jason was dead. Killed by a hit-and-run driver while crossing the street on his lunch hour. D.C. police were still looking for the driver.

God, Jason, what happened?

She closed her eyes. When she opened them again, the rain was coming down in biblical proportions and almost everyone was gone. She wouldn't be surprised to see frogs falling from the sky soon. She felt nearly alone in the world. Nearly.

Estranged relatives in Mississippi didn't count. But Karen Weathers did. Even if her beloved mentor was in a nursing home in Dallas. Abby tried to imagine herself in happier days sitting in her old college professor's office at Southern Methodist University sipping tea and arguing about William Faulkner, anything to mentally take herself away from her present location. It didn't work. She was too aware of the rain. The overpowering scent of the lilies. The pain in her feet. And the temptation to run screaming from it all.

"Miss Trevor, I'm terribly sorry for your loss. Your brother will be missed." The deep voice had a rich Irish lilt to it.

The speaker was tall, wore a trench coat and held a massive golf umbrella against the dreary weather. Rain splattered his outstretched hand but she reached to take it anyway. His grasp was warm and wet.

"My name's Abigail but everyone calls me Abby." She glanced up with her practiced "polite funeral smile" in place only to get a distinct jolt when she stared into unusual blue-green eyes that reminded her of dark Caribbean waters that could change to a deep emerald when the light hit just so. She took a moment longer to study the man's Cary Grant cleft chin and high cheekbones. But that's where all similarity to her favorite movie star ended.

His aristocratic nose had been broken somewhere in the past and his dark hair, misted by the rain, was cut in a longer variation of a military "high and tight." The combination made him a bit dangerous looking, but his air was open and friendly. Overall, the nose kept him from being too pretty, otherwise he would have looked like a chiseled European model.

Somewhere in her perusal she found her voice again, glad to be shaken from her pity party and wild thoughts of running barefoot like a banshee from the cemetery. His grip was firm and he had a bandage on his index finger. She wondered what had happened to it.

She let go of his hand and asked, "How did you know Jason?"

"By reputation, initially. I was a great admirer of his work. My name is Shaun Logan. We became…friends later."

An admirer of Jason's work.

What a strange thing to say. She didn't think her brother's work was necessarily well-known. Jason was a concept development engineer, albeit a good one, for Zip Technologies. Zip Tech for short. A cyber-security start-up. And now the man was staring back at her in the oddest way. She had a feeling she was missing something significant.

She'd never thought of Jason as having admirers, unless… Ah, color her embarrassed. Of course.

Her brother was gay. And this lovely gentleman must be as well. Okay, so she'd missed that entirely. She'd been too busy checking him out herself.

"I had no idea." That covered such a multitude of things about her brother—his love life and her present gaffe.

Jason had been very open about his choices but not his lovers. And Abby had adored him—not judging, even when her parents had, to their own detriment.

She swallowed past the emotion clogging her throat. "Thank you for coming today. I appreciate it. I didn't know many of his…friends."

"'Tis my honor to be here. I only wish we could be meeting under more pleasant circumstances." His accent was like sliding into a warm comfortable coat on a cold day.

"Your brother was quite famous in the high-tech world," Shaun continued.

She shook her head, still at a loss to reconcile the Jason she'd known and to understand this aspect of his work.

"It's not something you would have been aware of if you weren't in the industry, especially as his sister. You just loved him for himself, aye?"

Again, Abby swallowed hard as sudden scalding tears burned the corners of her eyes. There were so many things she didn't know about Jason's life. Had he told this man all the details?

She sighed. "Jason never shared much with me about his job. It was so proprietary."

He nodded and offered her a neatly pressed handkerchief from his coat pocket. "Everyone at Zip Tech signs a nondisclosure agreement. Applies to family members, as well."

"Did he speak with you about his work?" she asked.

"Only in the most general of terms. He worked on some very interesting projects."

Abby tilted her head. That voice. Shaun Logan could charm snakes with it. She'd be completely intimidated if he wasn't gay. She looked directly at him and smiled. "Jason told me a little about the new security project—Zip-Net, I believe it's called? He was thrilled and so hopeful for the direction of the company. I can't quite believe he won't be here to—"

She stopped. She couldn't think about that now or she'd never make it through everything she had to do today and the rest of this week.

"It's an exciting concept. Everyone at Zip Tech is optimistic about the future and they owe your brother a great deal," said Shaun. "He was a wonderful man."

"He was a pretty terrific brother, too." She bowed her head and dabbed at her eyes with the handkerchief. It smelled like the same fabric softener she used herself. She was struck by the incongruity of that as she felt Shaun's hand on her shoulder.

"If there's anything I can do," he murmured.

She looked up. There was nothing to be done now but grieve, and there would be time for that later, in private.

"I'd missed several of his calls lately. I assumed he was traveling. We'd been playing phone tag for a couple of weeks and I hadn't been able to catch up with him." *Or hear about who he was seeing?*

"Right. He was traveling with lab testing all last month."

"I wondered why we kept missing each other." She thought of Jason's garbled voice-mail message a few days ago. She'd only caught the beginning because the connection was so bad. *Buttercup, how are you?*

She'd assumed his call was more decompressing about his schedule. While he couldn't tell her much about his actual work, he could bitch about the insane deadlines of a start-up company and the unique personalities involved— all while managing to make it sound entertaining. That was Jason. And that information wasn't proprietary. She'd always been willing to listen. He'd certainly listened to her enough.

She fervently hoped Jason had had others to listen as well and to give advice. Others perhaps like Shaun? He certainly seemed to know her brother.

Could he tell her more about Jason? They were alone now in the cemetery under the awning. Everyone had fled the rain except for the funeral director and the limo driver. She dove in without really thinking it through, especially as she assumed he "hit for the other team" so to speak.

"I won't keep you any longer in this horrible rain, but I've really enjoyed talking with you about Jason's work. I'd like to learn more about that part of his life. Do you have a business card? Could I perhaps email you?" she asked.

He reached into his pocket and handed her one. "Nothing would please me more."

"Thank you." She slid the calling card into her purse, disinclined to leave but knowing it was time.

"How long have you been in D.C.?" he asked.

"I got in the day before yesterday. Wait, I guess it was yesterday." She shook her head. "My internal clock is turned upside down. I flew in from London and I don't have my times figured out yet."

"Do you live in the U.K.?" He took her elbow, helping her through the rain to the limo. The golf umbrella was huge, yet the swirling rain still found them.

"I do now…for the past three months. I'm a professor at SMU. This semester I'm guest lecturing on Southern Literature at Cambridge University while one of their professors is teaching English literature in Dallas. We swap apartments and everything."

"What a fascinating way to see the world."

"It is. I've done this in Italy and France, as well."

"Where are you staying while you're here?" They'd reached the limo and he helped her inside.

"I'm at Jason's. I'll close his condo while I'm in D.C. Then—" She stopped and stared hard at her wet right shoe before she took a deep breath. "I suppose I haven't really gotten that far yet."

She glanced up at him. "Can I give you a lift to your car?" She was reluctant to leave him now. Hearing him talk, she wouldn't have cared if the Irishman was reading the phone book. She felt peaceful for the first time in four days, like she wasn't going to jump out of her skin. It felt for some reason as if she were letting her last ties with Jason go.

He shrugged. "No worries, I took a cab."

"Can I drop you somewhere? It's raining so, please… get in." She stopped again and blushed. "Oh, my, I'm not trying to pick you up at my brother's funeral. Not that you'd be interest—"

She stopped and shook her head, wishing suddenly for the earth to open and swallow her up. "I'm sorry. That's not what I meant at all."

She felt herself blushing, and suddenly she was back in Ms. Martin's seventh grade class, stammering through her "How to Make the Perfect Peanut Butter and Jelly Sandwich" demonstration speech. On top of spreading peanut butter on her speech notes instead of the bread, she'd dropped and shattered the strawberry jam jar in front of the entire classroom. That day, she'd wished for the world to end, as well—for an entirely different reason.

SHAUN COULDN'T HELP BUT SMILE as she flushed again, a pleasant pink, to the roots of her hair. It was lovely. He hadn't seen a woman who got embarrassed and blushed like that in a long time.

The part of his conscience that was still active was mildly bothered by the fact that he was deceiving a woman who had just buried her brother. That twinge of remorse surprised him. Intellectually he knew how she felt. But the remnants of his own grief and loss had been buried for so long, they no longer clouded his judgment.

Growing up in a country filled with centuries of violence had not produced an idyllic childhood, nor had losing both parents to "the Troubles" of his homeland in a bomb blast at the tender age of eight. Years of denial had worked in his favor at cementing a manhole cover of ice over that dark mental abyss. He shook off the old ghosts.

He hadn't planned to introduce himself at the funeral and certainly not as Jason Trevor's boyfriend. He'd been ordered to keep an eye on Abigail, possibly even protect her—as needed—from the background. He wasn't supposed to make contact yet. Donner needed this woman's cooperation but that wouldn't happen if Shaun spooked her first. He'd considered the funeral as more of a scouting opportunity, but this seemed too good an opportunity to pass up.

Getting her to lean on him, trust him was the job he'd been assigned. Abigail Trevor was clearly in pain. Plus, she was in an unfamiliar city with no family or friends close by. He'd been over and over how to play this the past three days. The problem was time and how little there was of it. Winning her trust in such a limited time frame called for a wee…creative manipulation of the truth. Such as concealing, for now, the fact that the female Trevor sibling was much more to his taste than her brother would have been.

Maybe he should have corrected Abigail's assumption and told her that he was definitely not gay. But he had to insinuate himself into her life as soon as possible. So he let her mistake stand as the quickest way to get under her defenses.

Shaun was just grateful he worked for Michael Donner now, instead of his old boss at Storm's Edge. He could trust Donner and his motives. In other words, he could lie with impunity.

There was certainly no one around to contradict him. No one knew him or could question whether Shaun had known Jason Trevor as a colleague, a lover, or if he'd never laid eyes on the man until today at the funeral home viewing.

Jason had kept his personal life extraordinarily private, and Shaun had seen the change in Abigail's eyes when she thought she'd put it together, so he didn't set her straight in any sense of the word.

Seeing Jason's coworkers hurry past, most not saying anything to her due in part to the torrential downpour, he realized that right now was the perfect time to approach her. She was off balance, grieving. Not evaluating or think-ing clearly. Any slipup he might make could be more easily covered. Letting himself be "talked into" a ride was the perfect setup.

Except when he felt that niggle of conscience and a real surge of attraction that was completely out of place here. Then she was talking and he almost missed what she was saying.

"…it's just I don't want to ride by myself and it seems a waste. I can drop you at a hotel in Georgetown at least. It'll be easier for you to grab a cab that way in this rain."

Shaun grinned. This would be okay. It would be splen-did, in fact. "Sure and I'd be a fool to turn down a lift from a lovely lady. Just drop me at the nearest metro station. I'll take the train home."

What could be more ideal?

ABBY MOVED OVER AS SHAUN climbed in beside her. He was much bigger than she'd realized once he was seated beside her—at least six foot three. He wasn't imposing exactly but he was built like someone who worked out a lot.

Jason, even from the grave you snag the most amazing-looking men. What is that about?

At that moment Abby had a pang of longing for her brother and all they had lost that was so intense, a tear trickled down her cheek mixing with the raindrops. She turned her head away to the opposite window and saw that the limo driver had provided a couple of towels for her to dry off with. She blotted her face and offered the other hand linen to Shaun.

"Jason would have adored this," she murmured. "He dearly loved a good thunderstorm. They always scared me silly."

The limo driver swung around the gates of the cemetery and paused a moment as a maintenance truck rolled past. The plan was for her to be driven back to Jason's condo in Arlington. Zip Tech had made all the arrangements. She leaned forward to ask the driver to stop at a metro station.

Breaking glass and a soft *svit* sound thumped the leather seat behind her. The window beside her broke into a thousand tiny pieces, covering her back and hair.

"Get down!" Shaun tackled her, taking her to the floorboard. Suddenly she was facedown underneath two hundred pounds of heavily muscled male, her nose pressed into the taupe-colored carpet. All she could smell was damp earth from their tromp across the cemetery and the strange chemical scent of heavy-duty carpet cleaner.

More glass shattered.

"Damn it!" cried the driver, stomping on the brakes.

"Don't stop!" shouted Shaun. He raised up on one elbow and for a moment she could breathe. "Someone's shooting at us. We have to get away from here. Keep driving."

The back window imploded and showered across their bodies as the car swerved wildly before righting itself.

"Whatever happens," repeated Shaun, "don't stop driving."

"Which way do we go?" shouted the driver.

Shaun rattled off an address she'd never heard of in a heavier Irish brogue, adding to the surreal feel of everything.

Then he lowered his head again, covering her body with his and once again, she couldn't get any air. His hair tickled her cheek, then his lips were right beside her ear. She was light-headed from the lack of oxygen—and more. It was chillingly bizarre, yet intimate at the same time.

"Are you okay?" he whispered.

Words stuck in her throat. "No...no, I'm not. Why is someone shooting at us? Are they following us?"

"We're going somewhere safe."

He shifted his weight to pull out a cell phone and started texting.

"You didn't answer my question. What's going on?" Was this guy some kind of criminal that people were shooting at him in her car? "Why are they shooting at you?" She heard the rising panic in her own voice.

"Abigail, *I'm* not the person they're shooting at."

"I don't understand what's happening here. What are you doing?" she demanded.

"I'm trying to get us some help."

"By texting?" She didn't try to hide the sarcasm in her voice. Fear made her snarky. "I don't understand. Why are you texting someone instead of calling 9-1-1?"

"I need you to calm down."

"Calm down when there are people shooting at us, at me? And I can't…I can't breathe."

She was serious about that part. For some reason her asthma was kicking into overdrive and she was going to have to use her inhaler as soon as possible or she would be in serious trouble.

He shifted his weight, once again reminding her that regardless of his sexual orientation, he was a man and he had her pinned to the ground.

"Your driver is doing a fine job of getting us away from the situation. I'm making sure we have help when we get to where he is taking us."

"You haven't told me who you really are, have you?"

He ignored her question and called to the driver instead. "You doing okay up there?"

The guy nodded.

"What's your name?" asked Shaun. They were speeding along Rock Creek Parkway now.

"I'm Carl."

"Carl, I'm Shaun and you're doing great. Donner briefed you, right?"

"Yes, sir."

"Okay, I need you to take us to that address I gave you."

Carl nodded.

"What's going on? Why won't you tell me? Carl?" She turned her head to meet Shaun's eyes. "Where are we going? To the police?"

They were nose to nose and she could see a tiny scar under his chin. His eyes seemed darker up close than she'd originally thought, with deep green flecks in the irises. She stared, determined not to look away or back down till she got answers.

"No police. But 'tis a safe place, where we're going," Shaun answered.

"Why no police?"

"Because I'm not sure they can help you right now."

"And you can? Who are you?" she asked again. Fear was giving way to anger.

"A friend." The snake charmer was long gone; he was cool and businesslike.

She shook her head and turned back to face the carpet. Some friend. No one had started shooting till she met him and up until two minutes ago, Carl had been *her* driver.

"Why should I believe that?" she whispered.

Chapter Two

Shaun heard the whisper of her voice but couldn't catch what she'd said as he contemplated the back of Abigail's blond head. She was so small, he had to be crushing her beneath him. Yet he felt compelled to physically shield her until he was absolutely certain that danger had passed. He rose up and checked out the window before hunkering down again. Carl had left behind whoever was shooting at them, but Shaun was still buzzing from the adrenaline rush.

In his mind's eye he could see a bullet whizzing through the door. If Abigail Trevor hadn't leaned forward when she did, he'd be dealing with another dead body.

He couldn't think about that. He was surprised that someone had tried to kill her. He was expecting bribes, threats, intimidation. That was what his assignment brief had covered. The situation wasn't supposed to turn violent—not yet, not without any warning first to make it clear to Abigail what was at stake. This was more dangerous than he had realized, which made it all the more imperative that he keep her safe.

"Can you get off me, please? I can't breathe. I'm not kidding. I have asthma." Her voice was thin but firm.

Ah, Christ. It wouldn't do to save her from bullets only to have her die of asphyxiation. Careful of the glass, he rolled to the side and helped her turn over without cutting herself.

She took a wheezing gulp of air, sat up and coughed.

"Do you have one of those inhaler things?" he asked.

She rubbed the back of her neck. "I'm not sure. Probably not."

"Why not?" His tone was sharper than he'd intended.

She glared. "Because I changed purses this morning and I didn't think to put the emergency inhaler in my bag. I was burying my brother. I was not expecting to get crushed by a giant."

Her voice had a distinct edge to it now, but her eyes glistened with tears. She was more upset than angry. This had to be a nightmare for her and surprisingly, he felt bad for her. Again his conscience was taking him unawares.

He didn't have time for the demons of his own remorse and he couldn't do anything about her hurt feelings. Instead, he took her miniscule purse from the seat and dumped it on the floor of the limo. The time for being polite or charming was long past. What mattered now was looking after her as best he could.

"Hey," she wheezed.

Hairbrush, wallet, lipstick, cell phone, compact—nothing resembling an inhaler. *Damn.*

"I could've just reached in and looked for it," she protested. Another coughing fit racked her small frame.

"Quicker this way," he muttered. He tried to fit everything back in the impossibly tiny bag and was alarmed by the ferocity of her coughs. Naturally, the contents wouldn't fit.

Women's purses. He'd been all over the world, faced exotic things that had made grown men gawk while he stood unmoved. Still, a woman's purse seemed just a bit forbidden and slightly mysterious.

He quit trying to shove in the hairbrush and pulled his cell phone back from his pocket. At this point, he'd be better off doing something he was capable of—letting Donner know about the new wrinkle in their situation.

"What kind of inhaler do you use?" he asked.

"Huh?"

"What kind of meds do you need for your asthma?"

"Who are you?" she repeated, breathless with confusion and discomfort.

"I'm someone who's here to protect you and right now I'm your pharmacist. What kind of meds do you need?"

"An albuterol nebulizer and Symbicort." She gave him the milligrams. "I think I could use an EpiPen, too."

"All right." He typed the instructions into his phone.

Donner replied immediately and Shaun grimaced.

He studied Trevor's sister as she leaned her head back against the carpet. With all the shards of glass scattered about, it was easier for her to stay on the floor where she'd been originally. Her eyes were closed but he remembered their unusual color—like a single malt scotch.

He took the time to study her smooth, porcelain white skin. She had an exotic mole above her upper lip à la Cindy Crawford and features that were so delicate; she looked like a china doll—except for the wheezing that was growing progressively louder. He focused on her lips for any signs of asphyxia but they were still healthy and pink, not the slightest tinge of blue. Very soft looking, too. He looked away. Now was not the time to get distracted by a very kissable set of lips.

He debated explaining a bit more about what was going on but decided against it. She was struggling to breathe and she needed to be able to concentrate to understand the Pandora's box that had been opened with her brother's death. He settled for taking care of her instead. Over the years he'd found that actions tended to speak much louder than words, anyway.

"Do you need to see a doctor?" he asked.

She didn't open her eyes. "If I get my meds, I'll be fine."

He wasn't so sure about that. He reached for her wrist. "I want to take your pulse."

She didn't argue and that concerned him more than anything. He took her hand in his. It was small like the rest of her and her nails were free of polish. Her wrist felt impossibly fragile as he counted the frantic beats. Her eyes were still closed and he took the opportunity to stare at her once more.

Her black skirt was pulled up to midthigh; she obviously hadn't realized that yet. He couldn't pretend he wasn't getting an eyeful. He was so distracted by the fact that she wore stockings and a garter belt instead of traditional panty hose that initially he didn't realize he was gaping. He contemplated the red lace straps attached to gossamer nylons while he tried to take her pulse and glanced back at her face to find her staring straight at him.

Busted. He dropped her hand with a plop.

What was wrong with him? He didn't get distracted, especially in the middle of work. Of course in the midst of being shot at, he didn't usually see women in red garter belts with beautiful legs, either. Abigail Trevor was his own personal fantasy come true. Too bad it had to be happening in the middle of a job gone completely sideways.

"Your resting pulse is 120. That's pretty high."

"It's not a resting pulse rate when someone's shooting at you," she snapped, pulling her skirt down to hide his tantalizing view. "Can I sit up now?"

He moved back carefully to make room for her. "Sure, if you feel like it."

"I'll be able to breathe better that way." Avoiding the glass, she propped herself up on an elbow.

He was mindful not to focus on her legs or the way her outfit, that wasn't made for crawling around on the floor of a limo, strained across her chest.

"Please tell me what's going on." Her breathing intensified when she hauled herself to a sitting position.

"I'm here to protect you, that's a promise."

"You said that. And I suppose if you meant me harm, you wouldn't be ordering asthma meds."

He nodded as she continued to wheeze and his phone vibrated. Donner was sending more instructions. Shaun leaned forward to give Carl the new directions.

"Once you get your medicine, we'll talk."

"I'm gonna hold you to that," she muttered but again she didn't argue and given her earlier behavior, that ratcheted up his concern.

Moments later Carl pulled up in front of the Washington Marriott Wardman Park. Shaun wondered if he could get a severely asthmatic woman through the lobby without attracting attention.

The valet opened the door, no comment beyond a raised eyebrow to find both passengers seated on the carpet surrounded by the remnants of broken windows. Who knew what the man thought? He'd probably seen it all. Shaun and Abigail looked as if they'd been having sex on the floor of the limo, except for the glass bits all around them. Shaun tipped the doorman two twenties as he crawled out.

Glass skittered to the ground when he stood. He reached back to help Abigail get brushed off and out of the car. More shards fell to the pavement with tiny *chinking* sounds. Carl drove off as soon as the door closed behind her.

Abigail coughed and her eyes widened ever so slightly when she saw where they were. Squaring her shoulders, she walked with him toward a side entrance from the valet stand.

"How you doing?" he asked.

She nodded but didn't speak. Instead she held tightly to his arm, seemingly focused on making it through the door and down a long corridor filled with elegant chairs arranged in private seating areas. Opulent oriental rugs muffled their steps in this older wing of the hotel.

No one else was waiting for an elevator. Once inside the wood-paneled car, she leaned heavily against him and took more deep wheezing breaths. He was glad they were almost there. Her lips were no longer the healthy pink they'd been in the limo.

Shaun hung on to her when they exited and she almost made it to the door of their suite before her knees buckled. He pulled out the key card he'd been given earlier in case a "safe house" was needed, unlocked the door and carried her the final few steps across the threshold into the richly appointed living room. The master bedroom had a large balcony and sliding glass doors with a spectacular view of the National Zoo. The far more interesting sight was the large white pharmacy package beside the bed and the nebulizer that was already assembled.

Donner's second team was fast and Shaun was grateful. He'd sent the text only twenty minutes ago. Normally he himself was the one racing around like a bat out of hell, setting this stuff up. He wasn't sure how Donner had this task executed so quickly unless he'd known Abigail was asthmatic. But then, Donner was known for being prepared for every eventuality.

Maybe Shaun's job wasn't quite as secure as he'd thought. He saved that happy thought for another time and tore open the bag.

Inside were all the requested medications including an

EpiPen. Abigail was reaching for it and had the wrapper off before he said anything. She pressed the auto-injector to her thigh above the top of that stocking that had so fascinated him earlier and reached for the other items, as well.

She opened the emergency albuterol inhaler, using it twice before speaking. "I'll do a treatment with the machine, too."

She picked up the mouthpiece for the nebulizer and flipped the switch. A tiny stream of smoke poured out. Putting her mouth over the vapor-filled end, she started breathing in the medication. It looked as if she was smoking a hookah.

"You want something to drink?" he asked, feeling a bit like a voyeur.

"Water would be great. Thanks," she murmured between puffs. The change in her breathing from moments before was remarkable. He left her and texted his boss from the kitchen to tell him that they'd arrived and to take the heat for blowing his cover so soon.

His phone rang immediately. "What happened?" asked Donner. "I didn't even think you were going to talk to her at the funeral."

"It was too good an opportunity to pass up."

"I'll trust your judgment on that," said Donner.

"'Tis what you pay me for." Shaun wasn't absolutely sure he trusted himself on this, but he wasn't telling Donner that now. "Are you coming to explain the situation, or shall I?"

"I'll be there in fifteen."

Shaun snagged two bottles of water from the fridge. He started to go back in the bedroom, but Abigail's nebulizer was still puffing like a steam engine. Within a few minutes he heard it stop and her heels clicked on the hardwood of the bedroom floor. He stood. Abigail didn't strike him as the kind of woman who was going to wait long for answers once she was back on her feet. Better to meet her head-on. Maybe that way, he could stall until Donner got there.

He met her in the living room doorway. "I brought your water. You sure you don't want to lie down?"

She unscrewed the bottle cap and sipped the drink before spearing him with those whiskey-colored eyes. "No thanks. I'd rather talk in here."

"Let's sit."

"This is all very civilized." Her deep Southern accent came pouring out with no trace of the wheeze in her voice, but there was plenty of sarcasm. "However, I'd prefer we cut to the chase. Who are you and what's going on?"

Chapter Three

Abby stared hard at him, daring him to lie to her. Her breathing was stable and for now she was holding it together but she knew she didn't have a lot of time before the adrenaline surge wore off, jet lag kicked in and the day came crashing down on her. Still, as long as she was able, she was going for answers and right now she wanted the truth about what had just happened.

"I'll tell you everything I can." He took a long sip of his own water and met her gaze without looking away.

For a moment she lost herself in his stare. His blue-green eyes were that mesmerizing, changing from emerald green to Caribbean blue depending on the light. Then she remembered admiring his face when she'd first met him and he'd implied he was a "friend" of Jason's.

Had he lied about everything?

She glared, her blood heating for a completely different reason. Yeah, she was pretty sure he had. "Do you know who was shooting at us?" she asked.

"I have no idea."

"What's your real name?"

"Shaun Logan."

"What are you doing here?" she asked.

"I'm trying to protect you."

"From whom?"

"From those who would do you harm."

"Why does someone want to *harm* me?" She began to settle in her seat as she slipped off her shoes and tucked her aching feet underneath her.

"I'm not at liberty to sa—"

"Oh, bull." He didn't rise to the bait.

"Did you even know my brother?" she asked a moment later.

"I'd met him." He took another pull on the bottle.

"Did you sleep with him?"

He coughed and sputtered, the question obviously taking him by surprise. "I don't see what that has to do with anything."

"I want to know. He was my brother. You approached me claiming you were friends. I want to know how much of that was a lie." Her voice broke on that last word as she felt the loss and toll of the day begin to catch up with her.

"All I said was that I was an admirer of his work. That much is true. But if you need to know, then no, I didn't sleep with your brother. For the record, I'm straight, not gay."

Right. She'd pretty much guessed that when she'd caught him checking out her legs in the limo, but she'd wanted to know for sure. She studied him like a bug under glass, and to his credit he didn't flinch beyond that initial splutter with the water. Instead, he leaned back into the plush sofa.

"Some people might find your line of questioning offensive," he added.

"You said you'd tell me everything you could."

He shook his head and narrowed his own stare for a moment. Other men might have raked their eyes down her body to make their point, but his eyes never left hers.

He looked deeply into her face, reading her and letting Abby clearly see that yes, he'd been aware of everything—just as she had in the limo. He'd felt her body beneath his, he'd enjoyed it and he wouldn't mind repeating the experience—minus the flying bullets.

She wasn't unused to being examined in what seemed such a personal way, but it had been a while. She was fascinated and uncomfortable at the same time. She didn't want to think about how this made her feel. Certainly not now. She moved on to a new topic.

"Who do you work for?" she asked.

"Zip Tech."

She snorted. "The same company as Jason. I don't know that I believe that."

"Why not?"

"You're definitely not an engineer."

"There are other jobs at the company."

There was a knock at the door and he stood to answer it. Abby didn't know what to expect—certainly not for the CEO of Zip Tech to walk into the hotel suite. She'd seen Donner's picture before in *Newsweek*. Today he wore an expensive Italian suit and shoes that she guessed had cost more than her own designer ones.

"Hello, Miss Trevor. I'm Michael Donner. I'm terribly sorry to meet you under these circumstances. How are you feeling?" He reached out to shake her hand then sat across from her without any preamble. He was tall and almost as big as Shaun but fair-haired and not quite as buff.

She noticed that Shaun had snapped to attention when he walked in. Was this who Shaun had been texting from the limo? Come to think of it, she remembered him saying something to the driver about Donner, but she'd been too distracted by trying to breathe to notice at the time.

"I've been better, thanks. So what am I doing here *under these circumstances?*" she asked.

"You're Jason's sister and you're in danger. We want to help you."

"Why am I in danger?" This was feeling more and more like Alice down the rabbit hole by the minute.

"Your brother's work was very valuable," said Donner.

"I know nothing about Jason's work. He took those nondisclosure agreements very seriously and didn't share technical details with me. Not that I'd have understood them, anyway."

Donner nodded. "It's not just a question of what he might have told you, though. Our concern is what he left behind. You're his sole beneficiary—and the only one who might be able to access the files putting you at risk."

"I'm sorry. You've completely lost me."

"Jason was our top engineer on a wireless security project. His hardware and software designs were at the heart of Zip Technologies's newest product, Zip-Net. I believe his security protocol will revolutionize cell phone capabilities."

She nodded. Jason had been so excited about his job. She hadn't realized the magnitude of its significance till now. "But that still doesn't explain why someone was shooting at me."

"We believe the shooter wants something from you. Something that Jason wasn't willing to hand over. Something that may have been responsible for his accident."

"I thought my brother's hit-and-run was random."

"We're not so sure."

"I don't understand. What do you mean? And who's *we?*"

"Shaun and I. We don't think your brother's death was an accident. We think he was murdered."

"MURDERED?" ONCE MORE ABBY felt the world tilt. "What? Do the police know about this? Are they investigating?"

"Yes," said Donner. "The police are investigating as much as they intend to. We are as well."

"I don't understand. Why you? Why aren't you letting the authorities handle it all?"

"Because they don't want to believe there's more here than a simple hit-and-run. It's a delicate situation. Allow me to explain. May I call you Abigail?"

"Please…everyone calls me Abby."

"My name's Michael."

She nodded impatiently. "Delicate how, Michael?" Her voice rose on that last word as her composure slipped over the edge of the cliff.

"Like I said, your brother created a new kind of security protocol that's quite unique. I believe he's changed how all cellular and data networks will be designed and secured from now going forward. I also think he may have been harmed because of his work."

"Harmed?" She shot a look at Shaun. "You're using that word, too. *Harmed* is getting your arm broken, Mr. Donn—Michael. My brother was hit by a car going at least fifty miles an hour through a crosswalk in Dupont Circle. He was dead before he hit the pavement. *Harmed* is not the word I would choose to describe that, especially if, as you suggest, it was done deliberately."

Donner had the grace to look embarrassed as she continued. "I don't understand why you believe it was murder. Isn't the product he created already in use? The design is out there and you have a patent, I'm sure? What reason would anyone have to hurt Jason over a product he's already completed?"

Donner nodded. "While we've already rolled out the first generation of the product and it's working quite well for our initial customer, it's not entirely accurate to say that Jason's work was done."

"Why is that?"

Donner glanced at Shaun before answering. "We have another client who has asked for an exclusive contract for the first five years. Normally we wouldn't award a relatively new technology with such potential to an exclusive customer, but this is a special case because of who the client is."

"Well, who is it?" she asked.

Donner cut his eyes back toward Shaun then again to her. "The Department of Homeland Security. They want the exclusive in order to use Zip-Net for all their cellular communications security. It's an amazing opportunity. It would fast-track this technology into the stratosphere. Millions of dollars are at stake. Company growth will skyrocket. Assembly line jobs will boom just to keep up with the demand. And as the cherry on top, our national security will be better served than ever before. It's a win-win for everyone."

She watched him as he talked and could see why he was considered to be so charismatic. Despite her confusion she felt pulled in by the force of his personality—his mannerisms, his gestures. Mentally she shook herself.

"Your brother was handling some debugging issues for the program the morning he died. You can imagine with an operation this large, it can get 'glitchy' at times, especially when it's just going online. He was about to install upgrades to take care of that."

"Sure." Abby nodded. She didn't have a lot of computer expertise but she knew how easy it was for her own PC to get "glitchy."

"Up until then Jason hadn't been sharing the software upgrade plans or file on the company network and frankly,

I didn't require him to. Industrial espionage is rampant in this industry and after checking to make sure he had firewalls in place on his home computer, we let him safekeep the information the best way he saw fit. The fewer people with access the better. I see now that was a huge error on my part. We never expected anyone to resort to murder."

"But how can you be sure it was murder? The police seem convinced it was an accident."

"If it was an accident that your brother died right before turning in the updates, that would be quite a coincidence—don't you think? If we can't make those upgrades, the government contract won't go through. The consequences for not delivering the product would be catastrophic to Zip Tech and to this new protocol because of the blow it will be to our company's credibility. Any 'accidents' at this time would make me suspicious, but then for you to be attacked at the funeral? Bullets aren't an accident, Abby. Someone fired those shots on purpose."

"And your competitors would kill me and my brother to see that technology fail?"

"Unfortunately, some would. We're talking about a billion-dollar security industry that's about to be turned on its ear."

"I don't understand." But she did; she just didn't want to believe it. Her stomach threatened to rebel and her skin grew clammy. Everything felt so surreal. Jason was a lovable, geeky guy, and this all sounded like something out of a spy novel. How did he turn into a target? How did *she* turn in to a target?

"The next generation of cell phone traffic will be carried exclusively over the internet. Security isn't just one of the issues in cell phone communication, it's the *only* issue. Your brother designed an exceptionally unique product with an unbreakable code that keeps cellular traffic completely confidential. Unhackable. Homeland Security is so confident in the technology that they are willing to contract exclusively with Zip Technologies for security services. But in order for that to happen, we need the upgrade file, and we need to find it fast. There's an issue of a delivery deadline. We have four days to get the updates installed or this contract with Homeland Security is dead in the water."

"What kind of updates are you talking about? It sounds like more of a major flaw in the system," she observed.

Now it was Shaun glancing at Donner. The CEO nodded.

"The bugs in the system right now aren't just glitches, they're showstoppers," Shaun explained. "We must find the fix Jason created the morning he died, going in through the back door."

"What do you mean by *back door?*" she asked.

"'Tis technical."

"Make me understand," she argued.

"Many engineers put special signatures on their work. It used to be a vanity piece. Now it's a way into the system they've created so they can tweak things if necessary without having to go through all the security after production. It's a shortcut. We've got a major bug that needs modification and the only way to fix it is if we can have access to that 'back door' Jason created."

"What kind of bugs are we talking about?" she asked.

"The kind that will make the system fail…catastrophically."

"Oh." Her eyes widened as understanding dawned.

Donner spoke up. "Here's where it gets tricky and highly confidential. Zip Tech is due to sign that contract with Homeland Security and pass over control of the system at midnight in four days' time. Once we sign, we'll no longer be able to modify the program, even through that back door. Zip Tech must have your brother's security upgrades to make the changes beforehand—afterward, we won't have access. Once DHS signs off on the contract, government engineers with the necessary security clearances take over and we step away. Without those upgrades from your brother, the DHS network will be vulnerable to hacking."

He paused a moment, no doubt to let the implication sink in. A Homeland Security network that wasn't secure.

"Why not just tell Homeland Security the truth?" she asked.

Donner stood. "Zip Tech can and will tell if we can't get the updates in time. But once we do, the company loses everything. Not just a government contract. We're 'all in' at this point. When negotiations began with Homeland Security about Zip-Net, our company made certain modifications to the design based on the government's specifications. Based on those specifications, Zip-Net is no longer viable for anyone but that first client and Homeland Security unless other large companies with broad user bases also adopt the technology. Which is definitely what we're hoping for, but it would take time."

Donner stepped into the kitchen area and poured himself a glass of water as he continued. "In this industry, six months is like three years. We'd lose our market advantage completely. Not to mention our investors. If this contract doesn't go through, the company is finished."

"I know this is overwhelming and a lot to take in," said Shaun. "But you deserve to know the truth about what happened to Jason—why he was killed. Why you could be next."

"You're saying my brother was murdered to stop this DHS contract from going through?"

Donner nodded. "People have died for less."

Abby sighed. "That doesn't explain why someone was shooting at me. I don't have this upgrade file you're speaking of." She looked at Shaun as she spoke but he said nothing else. He just leaned against the living room side of the kitchen counter sipping his own bottled water.

"Are you sure about that?" asked Donner.

Chapter Four

"What do you mean?" asked Abby.

"I think you might know more than you realize," said Donner.

She didn't answer but her blood began to boil as he continued.

"You have access to all your brother's papers and files in his home office at his condo. As his only relative, you'll soon have access to his safety deposit box, as well."

"Yes." She tried to tamp down her temper and the growing disbelief that he could possibly be asking for this, today of all days. But a part of her was grateful for the anger that was snapping her out of the grief and overwhelming hopelessness of the situation. She put on her best Southern belle smile even as the acid in her stomach burned. "What do you really need, Michael?" she asked.

"Access to your brother's laptop. The upgrade file must be there somewhere. Specifically we need the password. Our people have been at it for several days now and haven't been able to come up with anything that works. His personal security system on the computer will erase all the data if we keep trying incorrect passwords.

"For everyone's sake, we desperately need those upgrade plans. We've been through Jason's files at Zip Tech's offices but we can't find the information we're looking for anywhere. Once the product is complete, you'll no longer be a target. Until then, we can protect you. But none of this can end until you help us find those upgrades."

As he explained, the ugly truth became obvious. Zip Tech had already been in Jason's condo looking for the file. Though he tried to twist things to sound as if this was all in her best interest, the man clearly had no qualms about blackmailing her to get what he needed.

"Surely he has a backup for all this valuable data? I mean otherwise couldn't a competitor just type in the wrong password until they wiped the system?"

"Yes, I'm sure he did have a backup…somewhere. Unfortunately, we can't find that, either. Believe me, our people have looked. That's why we need your help."

"So you've already been in his condo? Uninvited?" She smiled a particularly sugary grin and felt her blood pressure spike up a notch.

Michael smiled back, a sheepish quality to it that she knew was meant to be endearing. Under other circumstances, he might have been considered charming. He knew he'd been caught but he still didn't realize how badly he'd screwed up.

Her literature students could have told Michael Donner that he was about to be pulverized. She might look and sound like a pushover, but she had a reputation as one of those professors you did not tick off unless you had a death wish for your GPA. And you did not lie to Abby Trevor under any circumstances. Grad students called her "the carnivorous steel magnolia."

She'd fostered that notoriety in her teaching.

She could be a pit bull and once she was angry, even *she* knew it was a long, difficult road back into her good graces.

The way she saw it, Michael was all about Zip Technologies needing her brother's upgrade file. Oh, he tried to frame it as a step for the greater good—even for her own protection—but she was smart enough to read between the lines. He cared much less for her safety than he did for the success of his company. If he was truly concerned about her, he would have come to her from the beginning instead of waiting for the attacks to start so he could hold her safety hostage against the guarantee of her cooperation. Additionally, the way his people had broken into Jason's condo made her hopping mad and slightly ill at the same time.

Well, to hell with Donner. She didn't care what happened with Zip Technologies's contract with Homeland Security. As for her safety…well, that's what the police were for. Whether or not they believed the hit-and-run that killed her brother was deliberate, surely they couldn't claim the shots fired were accidental.

"He signed a waiver fo—"

Donner was talking but she didn't let him finish.

"Tell me, did that agreement say you could waltz into his home and take *anything* you wanted *whenever* you wanted in the event of his death?" she asked.

Donner looked a bit taken aback at being interrupted. After all, he'd graced the covers of *Forbes* and *Newsweek*. She had a feeling he wasn't used to women *not* falling all over him.

"Jason signed nondisclosure agreements and proprietary information clauses at Zip Tech."

"But no agreements to allow you a search and seizure in his home after his death? You're a high-tech company, not the Gestapo, but that's what this feels like."

"Ms. Trevor…Abby, I—"

She kept talking, just like she did in her lectures when

a student tried to interrupt her before she was finished making her point.

"I'm distinctly uneasy with what you are asking and what you've already undertaken without permission. Until I speak with an attorney, I'm not comfortable with you or any other employees of Zip Technologies entering my brother's home. I won't press charges at this point—but do it again and I'll have your people arrested."

"I don't understand, Abby. Someone was just shooting at you."

"That's right. And I have no idea who they were. It could have been your competition. Could have been you for all I know, trying to scare me into trusting you just to get into Jason's condo. I do have a question though. If Jason was so valuable, why didn't you have security with him while he was doing this upgrade work? You were awfully complacent to have such a valuable employee climbing in his car and driving away every night with the future of your company on his laptop in a briefcase. Seems you might have seen this coming. And if you couldn't protect him, why should I believe you'll be able to protect me? I'd be more comfortable with the authorities handling this. Why can't we call the police about Jason?"

"I have," said Donner as he came to sit across from her again. "They don't think your brother's accident was anything more than that."

"But surely after today's shooting in the cemetery, the police will reconsider?" She stared hard at them both, her anger still fizzing.

"Perhaps." Donner didn't sound very hopeful. "I've been dealing with a Detective Diaz. It might help if you spoke with him."

"I'd very much like to do that, I'll just get my phone. It's in the bedroom."

"Use mine," offered Donner. "I have Detective Diaz's direct number in my contacts." He handed her his cell. "He's the officer in charge of your brother's case."

"That's not who I spoke to when I identified his body," said Abby.

"There are many layers there at the department," re-assured Donner. "We'll step outside, if you'd like some privacy."

"No, I'll go." She stood and walked barefooted onto the balcony that overlooked the city.

AS SOON AS SHE WAS OUT OF earshot, Donner turned to Shaun. "You're sure you've got this under control? She can't be left alone."

Shaun nodded. "Of course. Though I want to know what the devil happened in the cemetery. That was insanity."

Donner shrugged. "I agree but I don't know if even this will convince Diaz to investigate Jason's death as any-thing more than an accident. I have no idea what he'll say about this latest incident but it will definitely be better coming from her than me. He already thinks I control too much."

Shaun raised an eyebrow. "You don't say?"

Abigail returned from the balcony a few moments later, shaking her head in confusion. The angry look on her face told Shaun exactly how the conversation had gone.

"Diaz says there's been quite a bit of recent gang-related activity in the area around the cemetery. He thinks that's what happened and I was just in the wrong place at the wrong time. He's sending out an officer to investigate at the cemetery, but he doesn't think the shooting is in any way related to Jason's accident."

She handed Donner's phone back to him. "I don't like this," she mumbled.

Shaun started to say something but Donner spoke first, pushing the advantage like the business shark he was. "Will you let Zip Tech help? We can offer you protection that no one else can. And if you help us find the file, you can resolve the situation for all of us at the same time."

"I don't want to but I don't see that I have much of a choice. Tell me why I should help you besides the fact that you're offering protection as a kind of blackmail?" she asked. "If I can even locate the upgrades how do I know that will make the attacks end?"

Shaun spoke up. "There are no guarantees. But Abigail, I'm certain the shooting in the cemetery was related to your brother's file. I'm also certain that someone has already searched your brother's home without you knowing it."

"Someone besides Zip Tech? Sounds like there should be a revolving door on Jason's condo." She sounded angry and he couldn't blame her. She had to be scared and completely exhausted at this point.

Unfortunately that was exactly how he needed her. He didn't want her thinking she could take care of herself alone. And since she didn't appear to know anyone else in town, he had to make himself indispensable. Still, it was obvious she didn't trust Donner and right now the jury was still out on how she felt about him. It wouldn't be easy to bring her around—and would it actually pay off in the end?

The biggest question was did she even know her brother's computer password?

Either way, she was clearly too upset with Donner right now to share any information she might have. Shaun signaled for his boss to leave, and Donner stood to walk out. He'd given his explanations, as unwelcome as they were, and was leaving Shaun to deal with the consequences. That was his job, after all.

"Abby, regardless of what you decide to do, I think it best if you let Shaun stay. He won't let anything happen to you. This is what he does."

Donner's hand was on the doorknob but Shaun could tell Abigail wasn't buying it. And Shaun was staying out of it until Michael Donner was on his way. He could tell she was on the verge of throwing something at his boss's head whether Donner realized it or not.

"I didn't ask for your help," she said to Donner's retreating back.

He was halfway out the door but snapped around to answer. "No, you didn't. But I'm giving it anyway. Please, let Shaun look after you. No matter what you think of me, I'm not burying two Trevors in one week. I won't be put in that position." Then he was gone, closing the door behind him with a barely audible click.

She turned on Shaun as the door closed. "How long is this suite paid for?"

"It's reserved for the entire week."

"I'll stay tonight. Alone. I don't want you here. I'm fine by myself. I want Zip Tech out of my life."

Shaun revised his thoughts about her similarity to the china doll. She was marble. Cool and unmovable. But was she unbreakable? Time would tell.

She needed more time or as much as he could spare before he'd know the answer to that. Donner was usually smoother and Shaun wasn't sure if there was any recovery for his boss practically admitting they'd broken into her brother's condo. Giving Abigail space was the first step, and being as honest as he could be. He felt the now familiar stab of conscience. So…telling the truth would be a stretch for him. "Right. I can understand why you want me out—"

"You don't understand a damn thing, Shaun Logan. If

you did you wouldn't have fed me that crappy story at the cemetery about knowing Jason and admiring his work. Earlier you said you had met him. Did you really? Had you ever even seen him before the viewing today in that casket?"

Shaun nodded. "Yes, I met him at a corporate function last month. And I rode in an elevator with him two weeks ago."

She stared at him and a crack appeared in her marble facade as a lone tear streaked down her cheek. She brushed the moisture away.

"Are you going to find who killed him?"

"I'm going to try, but my priority is to keep you safe."

"Okay. You're still not getting near his papers because I don't give a rip about Zip Tech's problems, and I don't want you anywhere near me. But thank you for looking into his death. Now, I want you out of here."

"I don't want to leave you by yourself."

"I'm a big girl—I'll be fine."

He raised an eyebrow as she stood. Yes, he had to agree, Abigail was very fine indeed. Unfortunately, he had no choice but to walk to the door or get into a tussling match with her. And while that might be fun under other circumstances, now was definitely not the time. He wasn't going to point out that there were two rooms here in the suite.

He'd just go downstairs and get the room across the hall from her if it was available and sit with his door open. And if it wasn't available, he'd set himself up outside the suite as her personal bodyguard. She'd never know he was there. He doubted she planned to go anywhere tonight.

At the door she surprised him with another question. "Donner said this is what you do. What did he mean? What do you really do for Zip Tech?"

He'd never felt queasy explaining his job, but under her

penetrating stare, he did. He knew he had to tell her the truth. It was the first test for him here. But how? Hard and fast like ripping off a Band-Aid or with finesse?

He took a guess along with a deep breath and gave it to her straight. Finesse would be wasted, anyway. There wasn't really a polite way to describe what he did. "I'm a fixer."

"Pardon me?"

"I fix problems. You know. Company vice president's son gets a DUI, I help keep him out of jail and make sure it doesn't get in the papers. An executive's mistress threatens to tell the Mrs. about their affair, I pay the woman off. I keep Donner, his company executives and their families looking happy and prosperous for all the world to see and examine."

Shaun trusted Donner and up until this morning he'd always done the job without a qualm of conscience but with this woman, he was uncomfortable. It was a unique and unpleasant experience. He had no idea where those feelings were coming from, he just knew he didn't like them. She studied his eyes, seemingly not nearly as put off by his job description as he had expected her to be.

"So now you get to try and fix me?" she asked, challenging him with her open gaze, all but inviting him to fight back.

For the first time today he allowed himself to really look at her, not just sneaking glances when she wasn't aware of him. It was different from earlier when she'd asked him about his sexual orientation. She'd practically been begging him to look at her then. So of course he hadn't.

But now, he started at her feet and raked his eyes up her body, deliberately lingering at her hips and chest.

Her cheeks were flaming when he finally reached her face. He knew he'd been baited and it was profoundly unprofessional but he couldn't regret what he'd permitted himself to do, particularly as it wouldn't be happening again.

Still, he had to swallow before he spoke. "There's not a damn thing wrong with you, Abigail. Not that I can see."

Chapter Five

She glared at him and shook her head. Oh, he was a "fixer" all right. Good thing she'd had a big brother who'd taught her a thing or two about men. Tears burned the back of her eyes as she fought to stifle a sniff. No way would she cry in front of this man.

"I would imagine you are quite good at your job, Shaun Logan. But don't think you're going to charm yourself into my brother's condo or laptop that easily." She shooed him out the door.

The expression on his face would have been comical if she hadn't been hurting so badly. Suddenly she was spoiling for a fight. One part of her knew she was putting off the inevitable—being alone with her dismal thoughts and overwhelming sorrow. Hearing about Jason's work, the importance of what he'd been doing, just drove home the heartache of his death.

Her brother hadn't told her about the government contract, but she'd known he was hoping for something like this kind of opportunity when he took the job. He wouldn't have worked his brains out without the hope of a fantastic payday or substantial job security. Zip Technologies had been his life for three years but everything that Shaun was saying rang true.

If Zip Tech failed because of something Jason had left

undone, even inadvertently, it would be another tragedy to compound his death. But she couldn't let go of her anger at the disrespect Donner had shown to Jason's memory by searching his condo. She wasn't sure she could ever trust him after that. Could she trust Shaun? She remembered the way he'd reacted when the shots had been fired, protecting her with his body. Was it wrong to want to trust the safety he'd provided?

With that in mind she dove into questioning Shaun as he stood in the hall. "Have you always worked for Michael Donner?" she asked.

"No."

"What did you do before?"

"Same type of work," he responded.

"And do you really think I have a role in this mess? I barely even knew about Zip-Net before today."

He pinned her with those unusual eyes of his and she had the uncomfortable feeling she was being sized up even though she was the one asking all the questions. "Depends on you," was his response.

"What does that mean?" she asked.

He moved toward the doorway and she fought against taking a step back into the suite, angry at herself and at him that she felt the need to retreat.

"Like Donner said, I believe you have information. Something you may not know you have from your brother. I need your cooperation to figure out what that is."

"But I don't have any information."

"I think you may have access to the password to his computer or the location of the upgrade file and not realize it."

She shook her head *no* but at the same time thought of last summer and using Jason's laptop. She did have an idea about the password but she wasn't sure she wanted to help and didn't know how to respond without outright lying. She'd known that she could assist earlier when Donner had spoken of needing the password, but she'd been so incensed about his having gone into Jason's home without permission she hadn't considered it.

She didn't want to consider it now.

So she did the only thing she could. She closed the door.

Or tried to. Shaun slid his foot neatly inside the door frame to stop her.

Angry, stalling and studying him at the same time, she was puzzling out what to say when the day completely crashed in on her—the funeral, the asthma attack, the shooting, the wild ride to the hotel and the awful revelation that Jason had been murdered. Plus she was starving on top of everything else—her body's defense mechanism when stress took over.

Food. She wanted it. Now. Almost as badly as she wanted him gone.

"May I take you to dinner?" he asked.

"I can't do this anymore, Shaun. I can't think about this situation right now. Please move your foot." Her stomach growled, betraying her and punctuating the request.

She tried to close the door again and only meant to glance at him a final time because now she was exhausted on top of being irritated. But those uniquely colored eyes bored into hers, more emerald than blue-green now, and surprisingly her irritation turned to frank interest as her resistance melted like a snowball on a hot sidewalk.

"I'm ordering room service," she declared, more to convince herself than him.

Forcefully breaking eye contact, she gave in to the toll of the day's events. She was totally out of emotional and physical energy to spend on this…on him. She didn't shut the door. She just let go of the handle and walked back to the sofa.

He followed her inside the suite. "Why don't you rest while I make arrangements for dinner?" he offered.

"If I go to sleep now I won't wake up for a month. I'd rather eat first."

"Of course." He nodded and picked up the room service menu from the coffee table. "What would you prefer?" His question, spoken in that lovely rhythmic cadence hung in the air as thunder rumbled outside. Rain pummeled the window and suddenly everything here felt too intimate, too close. Abby didn't want to be alone in a room with this man who set her libido to buzzing simply by talking and looking at her. In her diminished state of resistance that could be very bad.

"I think I'd rather go to the restaurant downstairs. Can we do that?"

"Whatever you'd like."

Whatever she'd like was a loaded phrase and one she wasn't going to dwell on. What she'd like was this man's hands on her body, a huge glass of Merlot, ten hours of sleep and most of all…Jason. Laughing, joking, taking her shopping. Alive.

But none of that was going to happen. Her brother was buried in a grave less than ten miles from where she stood. He was never coming back. The people who killed him might be coming for her next, and she had no idea who to trust, who to believe. As comforting as oblivion might be, if she had a glass of wine right now on an empty stomach, she'd fall asleep on the spot or do something incredibly foolish with her new bodyguard.

No way was she going to bed with Shaun Logan. Not after everything she'd learned today. And definitely not after he'd lied to her.

"I'M FINE WITH WATER." Abby sat across from Shaun in an opulent dining room overlooking the Capitol and watching it rain. She was desperately trying not to get comfortable with him. With that Irish charm, he was pressing a glass of wine on her—despite her objections. And it was only four in the afternoon.

"You just buried your brother and someone tried to shoot you. Have a drink, Abigail."

And whose fault was Jason's death? Shaun's? Donner's? Some mysterious competitor's? A terrorist trying to derail DHS? How could she know? That initial question more than anything had her sipping the Merlot more quickly than was prudent as Shaun drank iced tea. She was even ordering another glass after the salad, when she should have waited on the main course.

Lightning flashed and thunder rumbled, putting on a display that many would have paid to see. The food arrived when she was halfway through the second glass of wine.

"What was it like growing up in Mississippi?" Shaun asked.

She shrugged, wary of his attempts to make her open up. She'd shut him down earlier when he'd brought up the possibility of going to Jason's tonight.

She didn't want to talk to him about her childhood. She'd spent a lot of money and time in a therapist's office dealing with it. Lord knows after her parents' upbringing, she'd needed the help.

"I'm not sure what to compare it to," she finally answered. "My brother and I were very close. My parents and I weren't. And while part of my childhood was quite wonderful…my teenage years were not."

"Care to elaborate?"

She sighed. "My home was a difficult place to grow up in."

She knew she should keep her mouth closed or better yet, take another bite of the luscious steak in front of her and chew till the urge to talk had passed. But she didn't. Later she'd blame it on that second glass of Merlot.

"My parents always said we could tell them anything and they'd love us no matter what. They lied. When my brother came out of the closet, my parents disowned him. It was the spring semester of his senior year in college. I was sixteen years old. After Jason told them he was gay, they cut him off without a penny. I begged my father not to do it, but he wouldn't listen. Jason barely scraped by that last semester, but he graduated with honors and never set foot in our house again until their funeral. I never forgave my parents for that."

She wasn't sure what she expected but Shaun was listening with rapt attention, his own plate ignored as she spoke. It felt good to be able to talk, really talk about Jason to someone who wasn't being paid to listen.

"He'd been planning to get a doctorate, but he couldn't afford to after they took everything. One day he had an apartment paid for, a car, insurance, a future. The next, he had nothing. My parents even emptied his savings account. They called it practicing tough love. In reality, it was monstrous."

"You must have been devastated."

She nodded, took another sip of wine. This was better than therapy, better than yoga, better than jogging on that damn treadmill at the gym.

"I wanted to run away but Jason made me promise not to. He said I had to get a degree or I wouldn't be able to stand on my own without their help. He got a job in Dallas and when I graduated from high school, I applied to SMU. I only went home when I had to."

"Did your parents realize how badly they'd screwed up?"

She shrugged again. "They must have, but they wouldn't admit it. We couldn't talk about him without having horrific arguments. I'd always end up grounded or making my mother cry when I was still living at home, so the topic of my brother became the three-hundred-pound gorilla in the living room that no one would discuss. After I left for college my visits were so rare, we never spoke of him. It was as if Jason didn't exist for either of them anymore. They died in a car crash a couple of years ago and left the house to both of us. So while I do think they had finally figured out some of their mistakes, by then it was too late."

"You weren't exaggerating about a difficult place to grow up, were you?"

She nodded. "Everyone has hot buttons surrounding their childhood. As a result of mine, I don't like to be lied to. Ever."

"I'll keep that in mind."

"Do that." She smiled to soften the warning and took another sip of wine. "Enough about me. What about you? Where did you grow up? I've made this crazy assumption it was Ireland."

The corners of his mouth turned up slightly and he nodded. "I was born in Dublin."

"What was that like? Do you have family there still?"

He looked startled for a moment—staring at the glass in her hand, his expression unreadable before he recovered and met her gaze. "Well now, that's a conversation for another evening and another bottle of wine. On second thought, we'll definitely need something stronger to drink if we're going to discuss my formative years."

He smiled broadly but the expression didn't quite reach

his eyes. She took the hint. He obviously didn't want to talk about his childhood.

That brought her up short but it was just as well. She was getting too comfortable with him. Sharing too much. Becoming entirely too vulnerable. This could only lead to bad things.

"Could you excuse me for a moment?" She stood to leave the table and Shaun rose. "You don't have to follow me," she said.

"Nay, but I do have to stand. Surely you remember that from where you grew up, Abigail?"

She laughed and felt the blush blooming across her face even as she turned away. Southern manners with an Irish twist. Too bad she couldn't trust him. Even if she hadn't had that second glass of Merlot she'd be charmed. Exhausted and slightly buzzed, she hoped she wasn't weaving as she made her way through the tables to the ladies' room.

She pulled the powder room door closed behind her with the realization that she was weakening toward Shaun and needed to rally her defenses back around her. She couldn't let herself be sucked in by his appeal. Until she found out who was really responsible for Jason's death, she wasn't sure who she could trust. No matter how lovely the accent.

The problem was, in order to figure out who'd killed her brother, she'd need Shaun to recover that file. Although working with Shaun right now wasn't exactly a hardship, particularly when he was giving her the full-court "charm offensive" press.

And besides, recovering that file was the right thing to do. She might not like Zip Tech's founder, Michael Donner, but to keep the company afloat and to keep a lot of people from losing their jobs, Zip Tech needed her brother's file. Other employees' families' livelihoods, their lives as they knew them in this economy, were at stake. Jason wouldn't have stood for that. He'd known what it was to have everything ripped away.

She was washing her hands in the sink and looked up when a well-dressed woman in a lovely designer jacket walked into the restroom. Glancing up, Abby met the woman's eyes in the mirror, before going back to rinsing. Designer Jacket Woman smiled, then turned to lock the main restroom door behind her before opening her bag and pulling out the largest handgun Abby had ever seen.

Abby felt the blood drain from her face and knew if she looked back in the mirror, she'd see a pale reflection of herself. "Who are you?" she whispered.

"A messenger."

"From whom? What do you want?"

"It's not important who I work for. But my message is. No one gets Jason Trevor's upgrade file. You retrieve the updates however you like but Zip Technologies doesn't get them."

"I don't know what you're talking about. Who are you?"

"Someone who knows everything about you, Miss Trevor." The woman pulled out a photo envelope and dropped it on the counter beside Abby. Water droplets covered the marble top where Abby's hands had dripped, but it didn't matter when the paper sleeve opened and pictures spilled out.

Inside were photos of Abby in London, shopping at the market, walking alone on campus. Nothing very remarkable but the last three pictures made her blood run cold.

Karen Weathers in a hospital bed.

The woman who'd been more of a mother to Abby than her own after she'd fled her home as a freshman in college. Karen, who had helped Abby figure out what she was going to do with her life. Who'd been a university advisor, then a mentor, now a friend, and who'd been photographed in her rehab hospital room, all alone.

"I believe Miss Weathers has recently suffered a stroke?" said Designer Jacket. The question was more a statement.

Abby nodded woodenly, her thoughts a jumble. She'd just talked to Karen last night. Karen was fine. Abby was planning to see her in Dallas, after settling all of Jason's affairs here.

"Tricky things, strokes. A patient can be recovering beautifully, then turn for the worse so quickly and you never know why. It'd be a shame for something to happen to a bright woman like that."

Abby went from fear to white-hot fury. "How dare you threaten Karen. She had nothing to do with any of this."

"But that's where you're wrong. Everyone connected to you is now connected to Zip Tech. I'm only the messenger, Miss Trevor. Stay away from Michael Donner and his company before anyone gets hurt." She stroked a hand over Karen's picture. "It'd be such a shame for anything to happen. Get into your brother's files and destroy them. If the Zip-Net sale to Homeland Security goes through with your brother's upgrades, you won't like the result. I'll be in touch."

"Or?"

"Well, you saw what happened to Jason, no?"

Abby had known the words were coming even before Designer Jacket said them. Still they hit with a chilling finality. Nothing more was necessary as the well-dressed woman slid the gun into her purse, unlocked the door and slipped away, leaving the pictures on the damp counter.

Abby studied the soggy photos and looked up into

the mirror hardly recognizing the face that stared back at her.

What was she supposed to do now?

SHE RIPPED OPEN HER PURSE and pulled out her cell phone, frantic to hear Karen's voice. When they'd talked last night Karen had been okay—just wanting to be here with Abby so badly, though it simply wasn't possible.

If anything had happened to her... Abby couldn't think about that. Karen was like family. No, Karen *was* family.

The older woman answered on the third ring. "I've been thinking about you all day. How did the service go?"

Abby gasped in relief. "Karen, oh, God. Are you all right?"

"Honey, I'm fine. What's going on? Are you crying?"

Abby couldn't, wouldn't go into everything now. She'd talk to security at Karen's rehab facility after she hung up and let them know to keep an extra watch out. Upsetting the patient would serve no purpose except to increase the woman's blood pressure. Something they were trying to avoid at all costs.

So Abby told a different version of the events of the day, leaving out a few details and emphasizing the ones she knew would distract Karen from the funeral itself. And if Abby elaborated on a few particulars, it was all in the name of positive thoughts being good medicine.

She had to get into Jason's condo, into his computer and into his files without Shaun seeing her. Jason's upgrade file was her only bargaining chip, and she needed to get her hands on it. How could she do that? Her mind was reeling so, she almost missed Karen's words.

"So this new Irish friend of Jason's, is he panty-meltingly handsome?"

Abby gasped a laugh, struck by the incongruity of her thoughts and Karen's words.

"Yes. You could say that. He's definitely too handsome for my peace of mind."

"Good. I'd say you could use a diversion about now," said Karen.

A diversion? Of course. That's exactly what she needed. Abby knew one way of keeping Shaun distracted so she could get Jason's file without him noticing, but could she really go through with it? He had certainly acted more than a little interested earlier.

She wasn't answering Karen.

"I'll keep that in mind, but don't hold your breath," said Abby. "I'll see you in few days. Okay?"

"Of course. Whenever you get done there in D.C., I'll be right here or so they tell me. I'm catching up on all that reading I've been putting off for years." Karen's voice sounded wistful.

"You're staying positive, that's important."

"There's no other way to look at this. I'll be back and I'll be better than ever. Now I've got to run—or rather, wheel—to my next therapy appointment. I'll see you when you get here. Go enjoy your Irishman."

If only, thought Abby.

"Jason wouldn't fault you that," said Karen, and hung up before Abby could argue.

"Goodbye," Abby murmured to the dead air, staring into the mirror for several long moments before coming to a decision. She reached into her bag for her compact, lipstick and hairbrush, carefully applying the lip color and smoothing her hair. Could she actually do this right now? Seduce this man, this practical stranger, all in the interest of pulling the wool over his eyes?

For Karen, she would do it. She was the only family Abby had left. Zip Tech would not get that file.

"WHAT THE HELL HAPPENED in the cemetery?" demanded Donner, stepping into the light of the bare bulb.

"I'm…I don't know." The younger man was practically shivering in fear. Hodges had been an employee for eighteen months, but he lacked Logan's experience.

Donner smiled inwardly as his expensive shoes scraped loudly against the concrete. The abandoned warehouse had been a good place to meet. He much preferred dealing with people in this raw, direct way. Just cut to the chase. Much easier. Too bad he couldn't do it more often.

Hodges's voice was unsteady. "The rain was so heavy, I couldn't see, sir. She moved, and my aim was…off," he finished weakly.

Donner raised an eyebrow. "If your aim had been anymore 'on,' this party would have been over before it began. You almost killed the woman. What in God's name were you thinking?"

"I wanted to make sure she was scared. That she got the message. Just like you said."

"Oh, she got the message all right. Thanks to you, she thinks someone is out to kill her."

"That's what you wanted, right, sir?"

"Correct. That's exactly what I was after." Donner studied the man and felt the weight of the handgun in his leather jacket.

He really hated to do this, but it couldn't be helped. The police were involved now. As soon as Abby had made the call to Diaz, it was a foregone conclusion. This man could not be questioned by anyone else. Most likely there were casings left at the cemetery. Hodges had certainly been too nervous after seeing his very near miss to have gathered them all up.

Donner sighed. He was glad he'd had the foresight to treat the carpet in the limo with those special chemicals. Abby Trevor's asthma had kicked in just as he'd hoped, causing her to need them—specifically to need Logan. Everything was going as planned.

He grimaced. Or as well as this disaster recovery plan could go. He wondered if he had enough time to use Hodges for one more job before he had to be eliminated. There was a risk because the shooter could be linked back to him. But after his misstep at the cemetery, Hodges would be eager to make amends. Motivated employees were difficult to find.

Surprisingly his stomach felt a bit queasy at the thought. Still, he'd known this was the road he was taking when he had ordered the cemetery diversion. Hell, he'd known it long before then but this particular track had been necessary to ensure Abby Trevor's cooperation. Bad luck for Hodges, though. Bad luck for Logan, too. He would remain completely out of the loop on this deal.

Donner's phone indicated an incoming text. Reading it, he was glad he'd waited to decide the shooter's fate. The competition was sniffing around. There was one more thing that needed to be attended to.

"Despite these issues, I have another assignment," said Donner.

"Yes?" Hodges's voice was so hopeful it was slightly pathetic. Donner detailed the grim job. Hodges was most anxious to accept even though it was obviously above his level of expertise. The young sharpshooter had no idea he'd never get to spend a dime of the money being promised him.

"Same terms as before. Wait for my call," ordered Donner.

Chapter Six

Abigail hurried to the table and Shaun stood as she sat. She looked a little pale to him, not at all like the blushing woman who'd just left a few moments before. "I'd like you to take me to Jason's condo."

He held his surprise in check. "Of course. We'll finish eating and be on our way."

"No, I want you to take me now."

"I can't do that." He didn't have his backup team in place. When she'd refused earlier, he'd told his people to go to dinner themselves.

"Can't or won't? I thought you were all ready to do this immediately."

He studied her. Something in her expression gave him pause. Her makeup was flawless and there wasn't a hair out of place. Still, her eyes were glittering and he wasn't sure if it was from tears or fear. "Does it matter if we go immediately or in a couple of hours?" he finally asked.

"Yes, it does. You were so hot to do this earlier. What's changed?"

"Nothing has changed. But I don't want anything to happen to you while we're there and I don't have my team ready to go with us."

"What makes you think something would happen?"

He shook his head and laughed but there was no humor

in it. "Given everything that's gone on today, I'd have to say there's a fair chance your brother's condo is being watched."

"Are you scared to do this?" She locked her whiskey gaze with his own, challenging him with what he would have thought was a sexual come-on if he'd been in any other situation.

"What's going on, Abigail?"

"I need to go to Jason's condo. Right away." No doubt about it. There was a tremor in her voice.

"Okay." He studied her eyes again. Determined not to miss anything this time. "We'll go."

"Now?"

He nodded and she leaned forward, staring boldly back at him. Her eyes caressed his chest and moved lower, egging him on almost. But why? He'd agreed to do what she asked.

His body tightened in a surprising response.

This was all wrong.

He was aroused and trying to figure out what in hell was going on at the same time. Something had obviously changed her mind between the time she'd left the table and come back, but damned if he knew what it was.

"We're going but let's head to the room first. You need to get your inhaler and other meds. We're not leaving without those. And I need to make one or two calls—to let Donner know what's going on and to get some people in place so we aren't going in unprotected."

"Of course. Thank you." She stood and brushed past him, her shoulder touching his as they walked along the corridor to the elevators. The ride up to their room was crowded. Her breasts touched his back as they slid out of the paneled car. He took a deep breath. An hour and a half ago, she'd all but told him to go to hell when he'd suggested they go to her brother's—and he'd have laid odds on her decking him if he'd looked at her the wrong way.

There'd certainly been no sexual overtones to their conversation at dinner. Now she was determined that they go to Jason's tonight. She was absolutely coming on to him with her smoldering glances and casual but deliberate touches. It was bizarre. She hadn't had that much to drink.

While everyone responded differently to grief, he wasn't buying a sudden sexual urge as an explanation for her behavior. While he'd have been happy to oblige, Abigail didn't strike him as a woman who dealt with sorrow that way—more's the pity.

He followed her to the suite, determined to figure out what was spinning in that lovely head of hers before they left for her brother's condo. He wasn't about to take her into a situation where they could be shot at again when he didn't know all the variables. The way to unravel it was to follow her seductive lead, and while the process would be a pleasure, the aftermath wouldn't be pretty. She would despise him for it later.

ABBY WALKED INTO THE ROOM in front of Shaun, careful to brush against him again as he held the door. She hated what she was doing, but this certainly seemed the most expedient way. She had to distract him.

It wasn't as if she planned to have sex with him. She just had to flirt, heavily. And Abby had an A+ in flirting, thanks to her upbringing.

She turned as they came into the suite and was startled to find Shaun standing directly behind her. She suppressed a small yelp of surprise. He really was "panty-meltingly" handsome, just as Karen had said. But handsome or not, she wasn't sure how far she would have to take the "distraction charade."

The problem was, she couldn't have Shaun looking over her shoulder when she searched for that file in Jason's computer. She had a password and she wanted to try it. But Shaun had to get her safely to Jason's condo while giving her space, too. She needed him to willing let her do whatever she wanted with that upgrade file when the time came. So right now, she needed him malleable, which meant she had to seduce him. But this was only for the sake of the plan.

The plan she'd come up with on the way from the powder room to the dinner table. Once inside Jason's computer—if his old password still worked—she'd forward herself the file then delete it from his laptop...if she could. Lots of *ifs*. She wasn't sure if she'd be able to get that much accomplished or not but the first thing was finding out *if* there was anything even on the computer. And the only way she could do this was to get Shaun on her side. And the best way to get him on her side...

Well, most men's trigger was pretty simple. At least most men she knew. And she was fairly certain Shaun was attracted to her. So this was all going exactly as she'd planned, wasn't it?

"You're determined to go to Jason's right away, aren't you?" he asked.

"Yes, yes, I am." He was so close she could see that scar under his chin again.

"You're sure you don't want to wait a few hours?"

She felt his breath on her skin. "I'd really rather go now."

"I see." He stood gazing into her face and waited a beat. "Better get your stuff then. I've got a couple of phone calls to make."

She nodded and started to turn away before he reached out to her. "C'mere. You've got something." He touched the shoulder of her dress to remove a thread that had been stuck there most likely from their time on the floor of the limo.

He smiled. "There." He gently brushed her shoulder and she stood perfectly still as the touch turned to a caress.

She stared into those blue-green eyes, watching them heat, feeling herself drawn in.

Yes. This was what she wanted and needed…for her plan to work, of course. She reached up to touch his hand on her shoulder. Her gaze never left his.

He clasped her fingers, slowly bringing their hands to his lips. She reached up with her other hand to touch his cheek. She could feel the light stubble of his beard against her palm.

He let go of her fingers, leaning down to kiss her face and she was lost in the sensation—his lips against hers, his hands pulling her closer. She forgot for a moment about what she was supposed to be doing. And she no longer cared about the plan as he slid his tongue past her lips. He tasted like coffee and the crème brûlée they'd had for dessert. It had been a long time since she'd indulged herself.

She drank him in, wrapping her free arm around his back and pressing her body to his. Her other hand was still caught tightly against his chest. He explored her backside, pulling her to him.

She tilted her head, taking the kiss deeper and when he pressed her against the counter, she leaned back and wrapped an ankle around his calf. He ran a hand along her side, caressing her breast through the thin material of her dress.

He set her on the kitchen counter and she opened her thighs for him to step closer. When he pulled himself fully against her, tiny alarms starting going off in the back of her head. But his breath on her cheek felt warm and she ignored the warning as she melted into him.

He unbuttoned the front of her dress. One hand was on the front clasp of her bra and the other was sliding past her garter and up against the silken material of her panties when the alarms in her head started clanging in earnest.

She felt like a fool when she realized what she'd almost done. This was not what she'd intended. Not exactly part of the plan.

Distract him? Yes. Have sex with him on the suite's kitchen countertop? No.

She put her hands on his shoulders and gently pushed herself away. "No. I'm not doing this. I'm sorry. I got carried away."

"Right." He backed off immediately and she forced herself to meet his eyes.

Abby wasn't sure what she'd been expecting. Chagrin. Frustration. Irritation, at the least.

She'd been wrong to let this go as far as it had and she'd understand if he was annoyed with her for stopping. But his face was completely blank—totally cool and collected.

No passion. No irritation. Nothing.

It was as if a curtain had been lowered over the heat that had been boiling a moment before and she could have been refusing his offer for a coffee refill for all the emotion he now displayed.

Instead of being relieved, Abby felt let down. She liked to think she made a bigger impact than that. Her body was still crying out for more, yet Shaun appeared as if he didn't even need a glass of water to cool the flames.

She leaned back for a moment and swallowed audibly. "I…um…this was not what I was expecting."

He raised an eyebrow but didn't say a word. The silence stretched out. It was obvious he wasn't going to say anything.

The flush of embarrassment crept up on her and now she was the one who was irritated. Damn it, she hadn't ended up on this countertop alone. So why did she suddenly feel like a whore at the church picnic?

A little voice in the back of her head reminded her that perhaps it was because she'd set out to do to Shaun exactly what he'd done to her.

But instead of rattling him, he'd rattled her. Badly.

She barely stopped herself from shaking her head in disgust. *What goes around comes around.*

Karen could have told her that—wise sage that she was. So much for Abby's grand plan of distracting the man.

She'd managed to catch herself in her own trap. She snuck another glance at him. He looked completely unaffected. She needed the cold shower, not him.

Well, she could act that way, too. The past five minutes had never happened. He hadn't just had his tongue down her throat or his hands on her butt. She'd pick right up like they'd been in the restaurant.

"So what kind of calls do you have to make before we can go?" she asked, sliding off the counter and buttoning her dress as if this happened all the time.

"Are you okay?" he asked.

She ignored the burning in her cheeks. "We're not going to talk about this," she said and shot him another glance.

He shrugged. "Talking can be overrated." His soft Irish vowels and hard consonants made that loaded statement sound lyrical but she ignored the sexual tug. From now on she was immune to accents.

"Who do you need to call before we leave?" she repeated.

"Just a couple of people. I need to let Donner know

where we'll be. Plus I want my backup team there watching us. You ready once you get your inhaler?" he asked, studying her as she buttoned the top closure of her dress.

She nodded, refusing to let herself blush again under his perusal.

Donner had left them a car and the doorman brought it around. The drive took twenty minutes in the steadily falling rain. The scenery sped by but Abby didn't see it.

At Jason's condo she stepped from the SUV before Shaun could come around and open her door. As soon as she exited the vehicle she realized she'd left her purse on the seat but since she'd already gotten out the keys to the condo, decided against going back for it. She was nervous about this whole enterprise, plus Shaun's old world manners got to her. He used them to a terrible advantage— when he wasn't throwing her to the floor of limos or kissing her senseless on kitchen countertops.

Opening doors and standing when a woman left the table—those common courtesies reminded her of home and she missed them. Manners mattered to her and were sorely lacking in lots of places she'd lived since leaving the South.

Still, she had to resist the comfort Shaun's inviting demeanor offered. Besides, she'd learned from her parents that charm and manners didn't necessarily equate with trustworthiness. They'd abandoned Jason when they were embarrassed by his lifestyle and her parents had been two of the most charming people one would ever hope to meet.

While she unlocked the condo door, Shaun stood close beside her, without touching, under a big golf umbrella. The air smelled of Pinion. Jason burned the special wood all the time and the faint piney scent clung to everything even though it had to have been at least five days now since a fire had been lit.

She'd spent last night here, but everything was different now. A light sheen of sweat beaded her upper lip. Were there people watching now? Had anyone been there this morning after she left for the funeral home?

Once inside she walked straight to Jason's office and Shaun followed.

"I've got some ideas about the password." Abby sat at the computer.

"What are you thinking?"

"I'm hoping he hasn't changed it since I used his computer last year." She didn't look at him as she opened the laptop and powered it up.

"You knew what his password was at the hotel?" Shaun pulled up a chair beside her.

She stared at the blinking cursor, unable to ignore his question or the tone of accusation in it. "I visited last summer and Jason gave me a password to let me check my email. How many more tries do we have here before the hard drive wipes?"

"Don't think about that," said Shaun.

"But the hard drive erases itself if I'm wrong. We'll lose everything," she argued. Her palms felt moist against the keyboard.

"And if you don't try, we don't have access. Either way, we're screwed here unless you make an attempt." His words were harsh but still delivered in that lilting cadence. There was no arguing with his reasoning.

Mentally crossing her fingers, she typed *837321* and *BUTTERCUP* into the appropriate boxes—Jason's gym locker combo from high school and his nickname for her from their favorite movie, *The Princess Bride*. Together she and Shaun watched the screen.

Nothing happened.

The machine made a whirring sound. Could she have typed in the password wrong? Her heart sank as the screen went ominously blank.

Chapter Seven

As they both stared at the computer, Abby became hyper-aware of Shaun standing over her—his breath in her hair, the citrusy tones of his aftershave. She was turning her head, about to ask him to move back a step when a screen-saver photo opened of her and Jason together standing atop the Empire State Building at midnight.

She exhaled the breath she'd been holding—then stared at the picture and let herself remember. The lights of New York spread behind her and Jason like a glowing picnic blanket. Her brother had his arms wrapped around her waist and a tremendous grin on his face. She remembered exactly how she'd felt when that photograph was taken. Tired, exhausted in fact, but so happy.

Shaun took several steps back. She heard him dialing his phone as she continued to gaze at the picture. "We're in, Donner. What do you want?"

He cruised into the other room leaving her alone with the computer. She was a little surprised and had no idea how much time she'd have before he came back. It was now or never. Someone else would be taking over soon. Once Donner got hold of this computer, Abby would probably never see it or the file she needed again. She wasn't sure where to begin but clicked on the mail icon for lack of a better idea.

It was rather overwhelming.

There were more than five hundred messages in the inbox. Some personal, some business. Painful as it was, she scrolled down to the day Jason died. There were a hundred emails from that day alone, along with one undeliverable message—a bounce back.

Maybe because it was easiest, she decided to start with that one. What had Jason been sending that day? Who had he been emailing? Donner said he'd been working on fixing the "glitch." Could he have sent a copy of "the fix" to someone before he'd made that fateful trip to the office?

Shaun's voice was still a low rumble in the kitchen.

Clicking on the email, she read through the bounce code to get another shock.

The message was originally addressed to her. Sent at 11:02 a.m. on April 10, less than two hours before he was hit by the car. This had to have been one of the last messages he'd sent before shutting down his computer and leaving the condo.

There was a video file attached and she clicked on it. Jason filled the screen.

"Hey, Buttercup, it's me. Sorry we keep missing each other. Thought this might be the best way to catch up."

Instantly her eyes filled and she brushed the tears away. Just days ago, he'd been sitting right here at his desk and recording the video clip on his computer, alive and well.

"Next week we close the deal to sell Zip-Net to…
God, I can't tell you where yet, but it's huge. Told
ya it would be."

He grinned before leaning back in the chair.

"I've been thinking I should tweak part of the
program, and today I realized…there's something weird going on. Abby, it scared me. When
I got inside messing with things, there was code
that I didn't write in multiple places. I'm pretty
sure it's spyware."

He shook his head and leaned into the camera.

"I know you have no idea what I'm talking about,
but this is really bad. Zip-Net is supposed to
be—hell it *is*—the most secure product that's
ever been written. It's going somewhere that
absolutely must be secure and someone has put
spyware inside the program."

He was playing with a yo-yo as he talked—throwing
the toy back and forth and then spinning it. The same
yo-yo was in front of her now. She picked it up as he kept
talking.

"I don't know how they did it, but this morning
I've isolated the spyware and put a lock on it, so
whoever was doing this can't get to anything in
the contracted package. These malware codes
were buried so deep. No one was ever supposed
to find them. And the timing on this is so close to
the deadline for the sale. It's bad. Only someone

from my team could have done this. Nobody else knows the program well enough."

He was nervous. She could tell from the way he tossed the plastic neon toy as he talked. He wasn't looking at the camera anymore.

"This kind of spyware would enable one to listen in on every phone call made from the protected Zip-Net customer. When you realize where this will be installed, it's just crazy insane. Now with my lock on it, no one can get into any part of the program but me. I basically made a coded key for the whole thing and I'm freaked out enough to know I have to do something with it. I'm still trying to get my head wrapped around all this."

Outside the wind had picked up again and thunder rolled. She wanted to close the video clip and stop listening but she couldn't. Instead she watched her brother toss the yo-yo, then spin it out before tossing it back and forth to spin it again.

"I'm going in to talk to Donner today. He thinks I've only been working on security updates. He'll have a cow when he realizes the entire program is locked down. In case I get hit by a bus or something on the way to work today, I'm sending you the security upgrade file and the key. Just for insurance."

Abby drew in a sharp breath and almost doubled over in shock. He flashed her his trademark grin as he finally looked up again at the camera. She fought to focus and keep everything around her from going dim. If she stopped to think about the hideous irony of his being hit by a car less than two hours after he had recorded this, she'd collapse in a ball of misery.

Shaun walked up behind her. She hadn't intended for him to see any of this but she was too stunned to turn it off. So many unanswered questions swirled in her head. Some things made sense and some made less sense than ever.

She concentrated on Jason's voice.

"I put the file someplace special and deleted it from my computer in case someone else gets to my laptop before you. I haven't actually sent the file to you. You'll figure it out. You were so good at imagining things and you always were a helluva domino player. Remember the last time we talked about this?"

She keyed in on the last part of his message. She knew exactly where he meant. The only time she'd ever played the game. It was one of the few happy memories she had of their family together. Jason had beaten them all quite handily at the kitchen table. Her father had been so sure his son had the makings of a great mathematical genius. Daddy hadn't been that far off the mark.

On screen, Jason laughed.

"I'm talking like you'll actually have to sort this out. Don't worry, it's all gonna be okay. Call me when you get this email. We'll talk. Even if it's in code. Um...that's a joke, Buttercup. Love you."

The screen went blank as hot tears ran down her cheeks and she gripped the yo-yo in her hand. She hadn't realized she was crying till now. She still couldn't believe Jason was gone.

Pain clawed at her chest but she fought back against all she'd lost in burying him today. All they'd never share together, laugh over together, cry over together.

Someone at Zip Technologies was responsible for killing her brother. She was sure of that now—and certain that no one could be trusted. Not even Shaun.

"Where did you play dominoes?" Shaun asked, handing her a tissue.

"What?"

"I need to know where he sent the file."

She glared at him through her tears, a combination of fury and devastation behind her gaze. "I'm not sure." Even she recognized the lie in her voice.

Still he held her stare, refusing to challenge her on the obvious deceit.

"Donner has a lot more explaining to do before I tell you anything else," she said, growing uncomfortable under his scrutiny. "Like what the hell is going on inside his company. Someone at Zip Tech murdered my brother. Donner has a serious problem."

"That's why he needs Jason's file."

She turned away. She couldn't do this right now. She wasn't sure how much of the video Shaun had seen.

She knew he'd walked up behind her at some point but had he been listening from across the room when Jason talked about the spyware? Did he know that Jason had locked down Zip-Net? Maybe he did. Maybe that's why Jason had been killed.

She needed time to process it all. "Well, he's not going to get—"

The lights flickered out as something bumped against the wall on the back porch with such force that it rattled the window.

Shaun was on his feet in an instant.

"What was that?" she asked.

"I don't know. Be quiet." Shaun pulled out his cell phone and started punching away. The screen illuminated things enough that she spotted a candle on the shelf above the desk. She reached for it, feeling around in Jason's desk drawer for the matches she knew he'd kept with his emergency stash of cigarettes.

"Stay here," Shaun said, walking away from her into the darkness.

He was still punching numbers on his cell as he went. Jason's office was in the center of the condo. Abby stared into the inky blackness after him as her hand closed around a square unopened package in the desk. She'd be glad her brother hadn't given up smoking, despite all her harassing, if only she could find what he'd used to light them with.

She reached farther into the drawer, finally locating a book of matches among Jason's pens, pencils and paper clips. She peered into the darkness after Shaun, unsure if it was okay to light that candle or not. Her night vision was awful and her eyes weren't adjusting very well. She struck a match, lit the candle and suddenly Shaun was there standing beside her.

She stifled a gasp. He was so quiet; she hadn't heard a thing.

"What did you find?" she asked.

"Nothing good. My backup is gone."

ABBY LOOKED UP AT SHAUN looming over her in the darkness. The candle threw strange shadows on the wall behind him, reminding her of an old-fashioned cartoon character where the villain is looming over the victim and about to pounce on the victim.

"Gone as in 'left' or gone as in 'you can't get them to pick up their phones'?" she asked.

"Both. They're not answering and when I look out the window, I don't see their cars anymore. This group of condos appears to be the only ones with no electricity. Everyone else at least has a front porch light on."

She swallowed hard. "You're right, doesn't look good. What do we do next?"

They were whispering but the rain had increased to such an intensity, he had to put his lips directly against her ear to be heard. "We need to take your brother's laptop and get out of here."

She nodded, ignoring the tingles of awareness that shimmied down her spine. "Let me get something to cover it with before we take it into the rain." She grabbed the candle and crouched under the desk to scrounge for a bag of some sort. Shattering glass had her startling and bumping her head against the kneehole. Something or someone was breaking through the patio door.

"Stay down," commanded Shaun, pressing her to the floor with his hand on the small of her back. He leaned over her, a gun in the other hand. His body heat seeped through the thin material of her dress. She could smell his aftershave again or maybe it was a shampoo he used that made up the scent that was uniquely his. This all had a sense of eerie familiarity, like today in the limo.

"Stay here. Blow out that candle. I'll be one minute." His hand left her back and she felt strangely bereft.

Still clutching Jason's yo-yo, she'd gone to her knees with no protest but just as she about to snuff out the light, she spied a plastic grocery bag tucked under a box of printer paper, perfect for protecting the laptop from the rain. She tugged on the sack, determined to pull it from under the forty-pound carton.

More glass broke. She took a breath to blow out the candle when she sensed someone behind her.

She had time to turn, look up and scream before the crash came down against her head and everything went black.

Chapter Eight

Shaun heard Abigail's scream from the kitchen and his blood ran cold. He sprinted to Jason's office to find her on her back in the middle of the floor. The cubbyhole under the desk was on fire; the papers there were completely consumed.

What the hell had happened?

He pulled her away from the flames and checked her pulse. Her heart rate was steady and she was breathing fine. He turned to beat out the flames, hoping that would only take a moment—otherwise the building would burn down around them. But then he spied the blood in her hairline. He ripped off his jacket, no longer torn between dealing with the fire or her injuries.

He heard a noise behind him and turned to find two men in ski masks. Both held guns. One also held Jason's laptop.

Shaun slowly raised his hands. "What do you want?"

The man with the laptop spoke. "Get the woman out or die. Your choice."

Shaun couldn't be sure with the smoke, the masks and the noise from the fire, but the voice sounded familiar.

"Who do you work for?" Shaun asked.

"You don't need to know that. You just need to know you have the chance to live."

Shaun stared at both guns pointed directly at his chest and felt the increasing intensity of the flames behind him. Unchecked, the desk and drapes were fully involved. The fire had moved so fast. There had to be an accelerant involved.

It didn't matter anymore if Shaun recognized this guy. He and Abigail would die here if they didn't move soon. If it had just been one man with a gun he might have tried to stop this madness, but two?

He wasn't crazy. He had to get her out. He had no idea how serious that head injury was. Nothing here was worth dying over.

As he picked her up, a plastic yo-yo fell from her hand. Ignoring it, he carried her through the front door into the pouring rain without a backward glance, stopping only when they were well away from the condo under the overhang of the complex's clubhouse across the parking lot. She was still out cold as he gently placed her in an Adirondack chair on the covered porch.

A cold ball of dread settled in his stomach as water poured from the sky on all three sides, cutting them off from the world with a silver curtain. He knelt beside her, rechecking her vitals. They were both soaked.

Why wasn't she coming to? She should be awake by now.

He sat back and took a moment to pull himself together. Why was he so panicked by this? Why did she mean so much? She was only supposed to be a job.

Sirens blared in the distance, saving him from dwelling on that thought.

Who had called the cops already? Neighbors or his missing team? Whoever it was, he was grateful.

Abigail's eyes fluttered open. "What…what happened?"

His heart started beating again.

He was so screwed.

"Someone broke in." He pulled off his dress shirt, wondering if his voice sounded normal.

"Who? Did you get the computer? Why are you undressing?" She peppered him with questions between coughs as he tried to check her eyes for any signs of a concussion.

"No. They have it. And I'm taking off my T-shirt to clean your face."

"Oh…" Coughing more vigorously, she tried to sit up but he pushed her gently back into the chair before pulling his white cotton tee over his head. "Who's *they?*"

"I don't know. Do you always ask this many questions?" He didn't intend to speak so sharply but he was dabbing at the blood trickling down her cheek and still getting his own equilibrium back after almost getting them both shot in what was feeling like a bad case of déjà vu.

"No, I just… Sorry," she muttered.

The sirens were getting closer.

He stopped and looked in her eyes. "No, Abigail, I'm the one who's sorry. I almost got you killed for the second time today."

Her eyes filled with tears. "I don't really see it that way, you know. I think you just saved my life for the second time." She stared back and something passed between them. He wasn't sure what but he was in danger of drowning in her seemingly bottomless amber eyes.

A fire truck and an ambulance both barreled up the quiet street saving him from himself. Despite the torrential rain, the condo was now fully engulfed in the flames. Other residents were emerging from their units, as well. Umbrellas dotted the sidewalk.

Paramedics and firemen leaped into action but it still looked as if Jason's unit would be a total loss. Shaun located a medic and brought her over to check on Abigail and give her oxygen. The asthma had him worried and he told the EMT about it. The uniformed female put them in the ambulance out of the rain to get a good look at Abigail's head injury. Her hair was rain soaked but it had a lot of blood in it, too.

"It's almost certain you have a concussion." The EMT stitched up the cut as she spoke to Abby. "You need a nebulizer treatment as well for that asthma."

Abigail nodded as the woman prepared a treatment. "But your chest is still going to be tight for the next few days. You should probably come to the hospital tonight to be checked out," continued the paramedic.

Abigail started to shake her head *no,* but stopped abruptly and pulled away the mask. "I don't want to do that. What can they do for me there that I can't do for myself?"

"Is there someone who can stay with you? You can sleep but you need to be woken up every couple of hours to make sure you are okay. And if you start vomiting, or having any kind of vision disturbances or tingling sensations in your limbs, you absolutely must get to an E.R. right away."

Abigail turned to meet Shaun's eyes. "I don't want to go to a hospital. Can you help me at the hotel?"

He had a choice to make. If he said yes, he was signing up for more than just helping her with the concussion. He was signing up to bend his rules, as well.

That little charade he'd played with Abigail earlier in the hotel room on the kitchen counter had been a serious miscalculation on his part. He'd meant to scare her into telling him what was going on, not turn himself on to the point where all he could think of was how to get his hands on her again. If he went back to the hotel with her, he'd be looking for a reason to do just that. Something about

Abigail Trevor got under his skin in a way that had him throwing all his personal precepts out the window. Even though he knew emotional involvement on the job was a recipe for disaster.

She was still staring at him waiting on his answer. There was nothing he could say but "Of course I will…if you'll keep that mask on until she finishes giving you the nebulizer treatment."

Abigail nodded gingerly this time and slid the mask back up. The EMT didn't look entirely pleased but she'd seen enough to keep her mouth shut. "Okay, here's the paperwork you have to sign. Where's your hotel?"

"Here in Arlington," Shaun lied. He wasn't entirely sure it was safe to go back to the Wardman. But he wasn't telling anyone where they were really staying. Not that he had other options now. But the one he was considering was a little insane.

"I'll be right back," he told the EMT and Abigail. While she was taking her asthma treatment, he slipped out of the ambulance and made a dash for his car. Working for a security company like Zip Tech, he'd been thoroughly trained in the technique he was about to employ. It took less than three minutes for him to pop the fuse from under the dash and disengage the company's GPS system, thereby removing them from Zip Tech's tracking capabilities. He stared at the fuse box in his hand.

How had he ended up here?

Shaun never got involved personally or physically with the principals. It would have meant exposing himself in too many ways. Not that there hadn't been plenty of opportunities in the time he'd been working for Donner. With his particular occupation, there were always beautiful, unhappy women around.

While he'd been with Zip Tech, Shaun had been

propositioned by several. It was a bit of a job hazard, not that many men would call it that. But he'd never treated those women with anything other than the utmost respect, even as he was telling them *no.*

His mantra had always been, when a woman was part of an assignment, she was off limits and was to be treated like glass. Otherwise, it was just too damn complicated and very likely to lose him his very lucrative position. Yet, here he was disabling the company car's GPS system, and about to sign off on paperwork to take Abigail exactly where he knew they shouldn't go.

Had he lost his mind?

Apparently so. He pocketed the fuse and ran back to the ambulance.

Twenty minutes later, the nebulizer treatment was done and the EMT was putting away her equipment and giving them directions to the nearest hospital.

Abigail didn't say a word. She just slid off the gurney, bumping into Shaun as she did so. Her chest hit him squarely in the back. He would have moved forward but there was no place to go and turning to face her wasn't a good idea. But then he felt her swaying on her feet.

She was so close he could smell the perfume she'd been wearing earlier. He turned. There was blood on the front of her blouse. He immediately quit thinking about how sexy she was when he was reminded of how close she'd come to getting killed.

The EMT shut the ambulance door and left them standing on the condo's office steps just out of the rain. Shaun slid his arm around her waist and they made their way to the car, getting soaked yet again in the process.

"You don't trust anyone, do you?" she asked, fastening her seat belt over soggy clothes.

He startled, unsure if he was ready to fully explain the

why of everything he'd just done. It took him a moment to realize she wasn't asking about the GPS.

"I trust a few," he murmured. "But there was no reason to tell the EMT where we were really staying, now was there?"

"I don't suppose so. Are we going back to our hotel?"

"No. I don't understand how those men knew we were going to your brother's tonight unless they were watching his condo already. But just in case they followed us from the hotel, I don't think we should make it any easier for them." He drove out of the neighborhood.

"Do you believe me when I say the person who killed Jason works for Donner?"

"I don't know. Everything is on the table for now. It's important to reexamine what we know so far."

"You aren't sure?"

"Abigail, even if I was sure, I don't know who did it. So I can't just dive in without evidence."

"Where are you taking us?" she asked.

"Shopping." He pulled into the parking lot of a Walmart.

"What are we doing here?" she asked.

"Getting you new clothes. From the skin out. We look like we just climbed out of a swimming pool and we smell like smoke. I've got some extra things where we're going, but you don't." He wasn't going to mention her perfume. "I don't think you want me picking out your bra and panties, do you?" He wouldn't have minded. She'd be surprised to know how skilled he was at that particular job, as well. He'd sized several women in his work for Zip Tech.

He opened her door and she stared at him a moment, clearly at a loss for words.

"All right, Abigail, unless you want me to pick out your *polyester* pants, too, you better come in."

That got the result he was hoping for.

She straightened from her huddled position. "I prefer the entire leisure suit, thank you," she countered and scrambled out to follow him across the parking lot.

Chapter Nine

Since everything she'd brought with her to D.C. had been in a suitcase in Jason's condo, Abigail had to start over from scratch. Forty minutes later, Shaun was hauling multiple bags to the parking lot—groceries, jeans, two T-shirts, underwear, bra, pajamas plus a pair of tennis shoes along with toiletries, makeup and a duffel bag to keep everything in—compliments of his company credit card.

Thankfully she'd left her purse in the car when they'd gone into her brother's home. That saved her I.D. and phone from the fire, but Shaun didn't allow her to use her own money. He worried that whoever was after her might be trying to trace her credit card activity. His cards should be safe enough—he refused to share her suspicions that Zip Tech was responsible for the attacks against them. She was off the radar and secure for now.

"Where are we going?" she asked.

"Someplace safe."

She didn't ask anything else, which meant she either trusted him or she was exhausted. He was a realist and assumed it was the latter. He drove steadily through the downpour, grateful for a reprieve from her questions. Donner didn't even realize Shaun still owned this property. It'd be easy enough to figure out through tax records, but one would have to be hunting for the connection. It would do for what they needed tonight.

Rain dripped from the tall oaks while he wound his way through the deeply wooded lot. The storm seemed to be subsiding at last. The two-story house loomed in the darkness as he drove past the circular drive around back to the garage. He parked the car and punched in his code on the electronic panel by the door. The automatic metal door rose silently and a single light came on.

Abigail was quiet when they walked through the empty garage and into an enormous kitchen.

"What is this place?"

"Like I said…a safe haven."

"A what?"

"No one knows about it. At least, no one looking for us tonight."

"How are you so sure?"

"It's mine. But everyone thinks I sold it…last year. Even I thought so."

She smiled and raised an eyebrow, leaning wearily against an oversize marble-topped island. "How does that work exactly?"

"I signed the papers and moved out, only to come back from an overseas business trip to find that the deal had fallen through. I'd remodeled it myself and couldn't stand the thought of putting the property back on the market with the housing prices so dismal. I love this place."

He paused a moment, surprised he'd just said that out loud. He'd never spoken the words to anyone.

"I still own it but Donner and the people I work with assume I sold it. I've never told them differently."

She raised the eyebrow higher and he shrugged.

"This is not because I don't trust them. 'Tis just…I don't

really share my financial issues with people. They'd heard I was selling and assumed it was a done deal."

"Where do you live now?" she asked.

"Donner provides an apartment in D.C. as part of my salary, so this place is almost empty except for a few odd pieces of furniture." He steered her toward the living room while they spoke.

"The master bedroom is still partially furnished and this room, too." He pointed to the large sofa and entertainment center. "I keep some essentials here for when I need to get away from work for a bit."

He looked around and took inventory of the living area along with her. There was a large coffee table, a matching love seat for the couch and an end table. But she wasn't studying the decorating. She seemed to be hunting for something instead.

"What do you need?" he asked.

"*We* need to talk about what happened tonight at Jason's—and earlier."

Earlier. She couldn't possibly mean what had happened in the hotel suite? She looked directly at him, seeming to challenge him with her eyes. He couldn't help but notice how pretty she was, even with soot on her cheek.

"Do you want to get cleaned up first?" he asked.

"No." She crossed her arms and stood in the middle of the room. "Who were those men at Jason's?"

"I have no idea."

She watched him for a moment. "I don't believe you. I think they were people you work with at Zip Tech. They're the only ones who knew we were going to my brother's. You called Donner and told them we were going."

"That's a big leap." Even as he said the words, he knew it wasn't a leap at all. But that didn't mean it was the only explanation. As he'd said before, someone could have trailed them from the hotel, or been staking out the condo.

"No, it's not. I think your boss is responsible for my brother's death and you know it. You just…" Her voice cracked on the unshed tears. "You just don't want to admit it."

He wasn't immune to her distress but he couldn't let that affect his judgment. He had to analyze all the facts before he came to any conclusions. That was how he operated. "I don't know anything of the sort. But I'm going to find out. Please, trust me just a little longer."

"Trust you? The company you work for is making that extremely difficult. Jason said on the tape that only someone on his te—" She stopped.

"What did Jason say? On the video? Tell me, Abigail. I can't figure this out or help you if you don't tell me what's going on."

"How can I trust you?" She stared at him for a long time before seeming to come to a conclusion. "I'm wondering if you already know. Someone at Zip Technologies is responsible for the problems within Zip-Net. Jason thought it was someone on his team. He found spyware in the Zip-Net program. That's what he was working on right before he was killed. Not upgrades."

"He said this on the video?"

"Yes."

"What else did he say? I need to know," said Shaun.

"There was code there in the program that Jason had not written himself, embedded within Zip-Net. Jason said it looked like spyware and that he'd locked it all down until he could figure out what was going on."

"Is that what's in the file he talked about sending you?"

She nodded. "He sent me the updates that you and

Donner wanted along with a key code to unlock the entire Zip-Net program. He locked it down the morning he found out about the spyware in Zip-Net. Apparently that was right before he…died. He was on his way to talk to Donner about it and…" Her voice trailed off.

"Where did he send it?"

She studied him again. "I'm not ready to tell you."

"That's fair enough." He kept his voice calm but acid burned his stomach.

She was right to be cautious. He'd almost gotten her killed tonight. As much as he hated to admit Zip Tech could be behind this, there wasn't another explanation, not if Jason was correct. It opened up a whole new area of ugly possibilities that didn't make a whole lot of sense right now.

The company was depending on the Zip-Net product being unhackable and Donner was invested to his eyeballs in the new technology. If there was spyware embedded inside the program, there was a serious problem. What had Donner really been after on Jason's computer?

Updates? A key code? Both?

Shaun was ruminating over the possibilities when Abigail said, "I was in the ladies' room at the restaurant and something happened."

"What do you mean 'something happened'?"

"A woman came in with a gun and told me if I gave Jason's file to Zip Technologies, she'd hurt…someone close to me."

"Who?" His voice was sharp. A boyfriend? He was clenching his teeth so hard that his jaw hurt.

"Karen Weathers. She's a dear friend who had a stroke a few weeks ago. She's more like family really. She's in a rehab home in Dallas."

He took a deep breath. "Why didn't you tell me this earlier?"

"I didn't trust you earlier."

No, she'd just tried to seduce him in the hotel room to lull him into doing whatever she wanted. At least now he had an explanation for her sudden change in behavior on the hotel suite's kitchen counter.

"And now?" he asked. "How do you feel about things at this point?"

"Now, I don't have a choice. I have to trust you whether I want to or not. Retrieving that file is the only way I can keep Karen out of harm's way and get justice for my brother. I need your help to do both those things."

She stared at him, seemingly unashamed of her admission or her earlier behavior. "I don't think I'd trust you under normal circumstances, but I know you can keep me safe."

His training kept him from flinching. She'd only known him about ten hours and had him figured out pretty well, describing his temperament so perfectly it was painful. He wasn't someone you normally trusted but he could keep you alive or he should be able to. Unfortunately it hadn't always worked that way.

Gregor Williams and the scandal surrounding Storm's Edge were in the past but they still affected his present. Mentally he shook off the black pall. He didn't have time for that nightmare stroll down memory lane.

"So what do you want me to do?" he asked. He needed her to spell it out. He wanted her to ask him. For some reason it would make it easier to bend—no break—that blessed rule of his if it was at her request.

"I want you to help me recover Jason's file and the key code," she said.

"Do you know where they are?"

"I think so. Will you come with me to get them?" she asked.

"All right."

"Just like that? You'll come with me? No questions?" she asked.

He looked at her. Knowing what he was going to say long before the word left his lips. "Yes."

"Because it's your job to get the file?"

"No. Because it's my job to keep you out of harm's way," he answered.

There was a beat of silence. "I have one condition," she said.

"Name it."

She cocked her head at his tone. "You can't communicate with Donner or anyone else at Zip Tech until we get back with the upgrade file and the key code. That's nonnegotiable."

He bit his lip against what he really wanted to say and she raised her hand to stop any debate. "No argument. You want to come with me. Those are my terms. Otherwise, I go on my own."

"You really think Donner is responsible for Jason's death?" he asked.

"Someone at Zip Tech murdered my brother. Donner *is* Zip Tech. Either he was involved directly, or he let it happen under his nose, and did nothing. In my eyes, that makes him just as culpable." Her eyes were liquid but her voice was firm.

"That's a serious accusation. I've known Michael Donner for two years."

"I want justice for Jason. You and I both know the only way I'm going to accomplish that is to get the file before someone at Zip Tech does."

"What'll you do with the file and code when you recover

them?" he asked. "Some in your place might be tempted to seek revenge rather than justice."

"I honestly haven't gotten that far yet, but give me time. First I have to make sure Karen is safe. I'll probably turn the file and key code over to the authorities. But right now, I just want to sleep. I've had a helluva day. I buried my brother, got shot at and brained in his condo after being held at gunpoint in a bathroom, then got stuck in a burning building."

She did look exhausted. He knew that despite her tough talk, she was at the end of her emotional and physical rope. Still, he had to make one thing clear.

"Right. We'll do it your way. No Donner. No Zip Tech. But if I get in a situation where I think you're in danger beyond what I can handle, all deals are off. I'll do what's necessary to keep you safe and call whomever I need. No bargain we've struck is going to stop me. You agree to that going forward?" He was staring at her, working hard to keep his gaze impersonal.

"Who would you call?" she asked.

He shook his head, never breaking eye contact. "Not telling, but you can trust whomever I bring in."

She nodded. "If we find ourselves in that kind of danger, I would be pretty stupid not to, wouldn't I?"

He barely managed to pull himself from her whiskey-colored gaze before doing something completely insane.

Unbidden, his mind flashed on what they'd very nearly done on the kitchen counter earlier. He could almost feel her skin beneath his hands. His body tightened as he imagined what it would be like to have her on the sofa behind them now—her body pressed against him, his hands tunneled in her silken hair that had fallen loose earlier.

He shook his head again—this time to clear the erotic images. "Dumber things have happened," he muttered. "Believe me."

Chapter Ten

Abby watched him watching her and decided it was time to take a shower. A cold one. This attraction to Shaun Logan was the very last thing she needed. She was vulnerable, exhausted and hurting while he was charming, beautiful and trouble with a capital *T*. Sinking into him for some mindless oblivion would be entirely too easy.

She broke eye contact and gathered her purchases from Walmart. "I need to get cleaned up. Where can I bathe?"

Shaun pointed to a staircase and led the way. She followed, entirely too aware of the way he filled out his slacks and damp dress shirt. At the top of the stairs, they passed two empty rooms. He stopped at the end of the hall before a bedroom that was fully furnished with a four-poster bed, mirrored dresser, captain's desk and an overstuffed chair.

The bathroom was like something out of a luxury hotel with a six-foot Jacuzzi tub and a television built into the opposite wall. Abby felt her eyebrows hitting her hairline.

"Wow, Shaun. This is pretty amazing. You don't exactly strike me as the Jacuzzi type."

The corner of his mouth tilted up in a smile. "That bathtub is a long story. I lost a bet but discovered I didn't mind that much. Truth be told, 'tis rather tremendous, actually."

He laughed and shook his head in what appeared to be genuine disbelief. "Who'd have thought? Make yourself at home. There are towels, shampoo and such. I keep a few essentials here. Just let me get some dry clothes and it's all yours. I'll shower in one of the others."

"But this is your room," she argued.

"It's yours tonight. I'll take the sofa downstairs. Feel free to use anything you need." He cruised into the walk-in closet while she looked around the palatial bathroom. "The EMT said you can't sleep for a while but there's no reason you can't be comfortable."

He left her and fifteen minutes later she was chin deep in the Jacuzzi's frothing bubbles. Getting her hair clean had been a challenge. She'd had to lather it up three times in the high-tech shower to rid herself of the smoke smell but now she was watching sandalwood-scented water swirl about in a tub the size of an Olympic swimming pool. She leaned against a padded bath-pillow, closed her eyes and smiled—trying to imagine Shaun lounging in the water like this. That must have been some bet he'd lost.

Instantly the mental picture was there. Dripping wet biceps and washboard abs covered in swirling water. For a few moments she let her mind wander…everywhere. Sexual fantasies might not be the answer to her problems, but they were a lovely escape. At least for a little while.

What was she doing here and how in the world had she ended up in Shaun Logan's pimped-out bathtub?

Eleven hours ago she'd been at her brother's funeral and hadn't known Shaun existed. Ten hours ago someone had been shooting at her. Nine hours ago she'd been recovering from an asthma attack and talking with Michael Donner. Three hours ago she'd been in a burning condo.

Now no one knew where she was. No one knew what had become of her. When had everything slipped so completely out of her control?

SHAUN STOOD UNDER THE STEAMING hot spray and wondered how everything had slipped so completely out of his control. There was no doubt about when it had happened. At the same moment he'd started bending his rules. Here was further proof of how far he'd fallen down the slippery slope.

He never brought assets home. This was his last place of utter peace. Now there was one in his bedroom, in his bathtub for God's sake. He finished his shower quickly. He wasn't bending his rules, he was shattering them. As he stepped out of the marble enclosure to towel off, his cell phone rang—Donner's special ringtone.

The man paid Shaun's considerable salary and Shaun wasn't going to ignore his boss, despite what he'd said to Abigail. He wasn't ready to break that rule, as well. You told the principal whatever they wanted to hear in order to gain their cooperation, or that's how Shaun justified himself as he once again ignored his conscience and knotted the bath sheet around his waist before answering the phone.

Donner normally didn't get rattled but he was now.

"Logan, what the hell is going on? Where are you? Is Abby Trevor with you?"

Shaun still didn't want to believe Donner had anything to do with Jason's death but he couldn't ignore the fact that when he'd told his boss and backup where they were going, Abby'd ended up knocked unconscious and he'd had two guns pointed at his chest. That was why he had disengaged the GPS before they left Trevor's parking lot.

"Abigail's with me. She's okay. We're just back from her

brother's condo." He explained about the break-in, the fire and his missing team.

"Interesting that she knew the password all along," said Donner.

A chill slid down Shaun's spine when he didn't ask about the fire, the missing backup or those men who'd held them at gunpoint. Was that because Donner already knew or because he didn't care? Either explanation was a fairly serious indictment of the man.

"She accessed a video from Jason."

"A video? What did it say?" asked Donner.

"I don't know. I only heard the end of it when Jason was telling her where the upgrade file was. Apparently he was worried someone might get to his computer and to the email he'd sent her so he crafted a bit of a scavenger hunt. He was giving her clues on the video right before the break-in."

He wasn't sure why he didn't confront Donner right then about the spyware. Maybe because he'd promised Abigail he wouldn't talk to the man at all, but he consciously chose not to go into the spyware or key code issue. It felt important to keep that information to himself.

"I have to have that file, Shaun. Now it's more important than ever. We can't fix Zip-Net and this contract with Homeland Security is dead in the water if we don't."

"I understand."

"Does the woman know where the upgrade file is?"

"Yes, but she's not telling. Like I said, Jason hid them somewhere. She's convinced someone at Zip Tech is responsible for her brother's murder."

"Well, you know that's bull."

"Do I?" asked Shaun.

"Of course." Donner's voice was smooth and convincing. "I need you to unwind the puzzle, man. You're my fixer and this is what I pay you for. Work your magic on that woman and do whatever it takes. I don't care about consequences. I need that file."

Whatever it takes? This wasn't the Michael Donner that Shaun knew.

Shaun didn't use people; he never had. And despite his job description, Donner had never asked him to forget consequences. Shaun's whole purpose at Zip Tech was about avoiding consequences. That's why he'd been hired. What was going on?

Michael was always conscious of his public image. This felt like Storm's Edge and the disaster in Iraq all over again. Shaun couldn't believe the irony. Didn't want to accept it. Donner hadn't even mentioned the key code or Jason having locked down Zip-Net. He had to know about the lock, so why wasn't he asking about the key code? It all seemed very wrong. The key code was more important than the upgrade file at this point.

Was Abigail right? Was Donner responsible for Jason's death or was he completely clueless about everything going on? Shaun had to buy time to figure it out. He couldn't lie directly to his boss but there was no way he was mentioning the spyware now.

Still, he was about to start a very dangerous game. If he was guilty, Donner had far too many resources and fail-safes for Shaun to outrun him. He had more bells and whistles in wireless communication than Shaun could ever hope to understand. If Donner thought he was being played, he could have them hunted down and crushed if he wanted to. Shaun and Abigail would never know what hit them if they started without marshaling their own resources and aroused Donner's suspicion.

But Shaun had some of his own resources he could

call on, as well. He'd play along until he had everything unwound.

"Okay, Michael. But she doesn't want me contacting you while I'm with her. She doesn't trust you." He heard Donner's low chuckle over the phone.

"And you couldn't convince her I'm completely trust-worthy? I'm surprised at you."

Shaun forced a levity into his voice he didn't feel. "There's just so much I can do before I start sounding like your fan club president. I'll contact you when I can to let you know where we are. For now it'd be better if you backed off and gave us room. I don't want her spooked any-more than she already is. Why don't you work the police on your end to find out about the fire? I got her out of there before the cops could start asking a lot of questions."

There was a pause and Shaun knew in his gut—his boss wasn't going to contact the authorities. He'd been so mistaken about Donner.

About everything.

Suddenly it seemed extraordinarily important to get off the phone as quickly as possible. Donner hated being out of the loop and could be tracing this call right now just to satisfy his curiosity about where Shaun and Abigail were spending the night.

The knowledge had him reeling. He was back in a long hallway hearing a girl's screams, the clinical smells and sounds of a hospital. Fire, explosions, darkness and pain.

Later finding that she'd disappeared completely off the face of the earth. He'd known then what the people he re-spected were capable of and he'd never forgotten the way it had made him feel. Betrayed, grasping for something to hold on to. Something to believe in.

Donner's voice brought him back to the present nightmare. "All right, but you stay in touch. I need that file ASAP. Remember, we sign the contract in four days."

How could he forget?

Shaun hit End and pulled on his clothes, feeling as if the top of his head was about to fly off. Four days to figure out why a man he trusted and looked up to had possibly had one of his own employees killed. It didn't make sense. Donner stood more to lose than anyone if the Homeland Security contract fell through for Zip-Net.

How did Shaun talk to Abigail about the conversation he'd just had? She'd asked him not to communicate with Donner at all if he wanted to come with her to get the file. Telling her that he'd just told his boss almost everything seemed like a good way to get his ass booted to the curb, even if he told her the conversation had convinced him that she'd been right.

He had a sick feeling that Donner was indeed responsible for Jason's death. But nothing about it made sense. He still didn't know what was going on or why. And the last thing he wanted was for her to fly off the handle and run off on her own, as she'd threatened.

So, for now, he'd say nothing to her. That might be a mistake as well, but this seemed to be his day for screwing up his life and breaking all his own rules.

Besides, words had never meant much to him; it had always been what you did that made the difference. How you stood for what you said you cared about. It defined who you were. People trusted what they saw you do, not what you said you'd do. If someone didn't trust him, he'd always found that showing them rather than telling them was more important.

That could work both ways here. He'd have to show her that she could trust him and hope that she really knew where Jason's file and the key code were. If not, they were both in more trouble than his considerable skills could deliver them from.

Chapter Eleven

Barefooted, Shaun wandered downstairs to the fridge. He wasn't hungry but he opened the stainless door anyway. He had beer, wine, Gatorade and one can of soda. The beer was tempting but that wasn't a possibility when he was working.

Deciding on a pot of coffee instead, he turned when Abigail came into the kitchen. Her hair was damp and piled high on her head in a clip, drying in wild curls around her cheeks. She'd put on his robe over her new pj's. He fought against staring at how the silk garment enveloped her while still accentuating her generous curves. Forgotten till now, the designer robe had been hanging on the back of his master bathroom door—a gift from a former lover who hadn't known his tastes very well.

"I didn't want to put on my new clothes since I was going to need them tomorrow," she explained. "I took you at your word and borrowed this."

How was it that the robe swallowed her but still managed to get him hot at the same time? That was simple. He'd been on top of her more than once today plus the interlude with her on that damn kitchen counter he was going to dream about. It wasn't much of a leap to imagine exactly how she'd feel against him if she wasn't wearing anything at all.

He turned abruptly to the refrigerator again. Bringing her home with him had been a horrible idea. "Can I get you something to drink?" he asked, opening the freezer compartment. "I'm about to make coffee, it's caffeinated."

"No, just water for now. My throat is terribly dry from the smoke."

"Of course." He should probably have some ice water himself. He could just dump it down the front of his jeans.

"How's your head feeling?" He got her a glass.

She wobbled her hand back and forth. "So-so. Do you have any ibuprofen?"

"I don't know. I may have cleaned out all that kind of thing when I was moving the first time. I'll check and see."

She nodded, rubbing the back of her neck and shoulders. "What's up with your neck?"

"I don't know…I think I twisted something funny when I was under the desk, just before I got hit." She tried to sidle onto a bar stool but winced as she sat.

He handed her the water and walked behind her. Placing his palms on her shoulders under the robe, he felt a knot in the muscles along with the heat from her skin.

Putting his hands on her like this was probably a mistake too, but he could just add it to the list of mistakes he seemed to be making where Abigail was concerned. Besides, she was hurting and he could fix it. He'd had the training. And he desperately needed to fix something about this crazy, screwed up day.

He pressed his thumbs along each side of her spinal column starting at her hairline.

She moaned out loud. "Ohhh, that feels amazing."

Yes, it does.

Her skin was just as smooth as he'd imagined. Slowly

he turned her head from side to side before kneading the muscles along the base of her neck and back into her scalp. The knot was loosening already.

He pushed harder. The soft sounds she made had his mouth going dry and his body tensing up. He closed his eyes and took a deep breath as she sank into the bar stool armrest. The back of her head was almost touching the middle of his chest.

He could smell his bath soap on her. The scent was different on her body—or maybe it was just her scent in general. She made little mewing sounds in her throat as he rubbed her neck. He knew it had nothing to do with sex in her mind but she was definitely turning him on.

This was such a huge mistake.

He dropped his hands. "I think that's got you taken care of."

She sat up slowly, turning her head this way and that. "Yes. It is…much better. Thanks so much. That's…that's remarkable."

She swiveled on the seat to face him, but he turned away to busy himself with the coffee before he did anything insane like bury his head in her hair or pull her into his arms.

"No problem," he muttered.

"So how are we going to do this?" Abigail asked, sliding off the bar stool.

"Pardon me?" Shaun's one-track mind was still reeling in the wrong direction.

"How are we going to stay awake?"

"Oh. You don't have to. The EMT said you could sleep, you just have to be woken up every couple of hours. I'll be setting an alarm."

"That doesn't seem very fair for you to have to stay awake while I'm sleeping." She stifled a yawn, stretching as she spoke. His robe, too big for her, gapped open to reveal a lacy camisole underneath. He suddenly had a whole new appreciation for the lingerie department at Walmart.

"It's okay. I'll doze. I don't need a lot of sleep. Besides, you're practically out on your feet. Your head will feel better this way, too. Go on up and I'll look for that ibuprofen."

He followed her, grateful she would be upstairs. After his conversation with Donner, he felt so mixed up, so upside down. The farther away he was from Abigail right now the better.

He rifled through the medicine cabinet, spied the pain reliever and found her at the bedroom window, staring into the night. The drapes were open, moonlight bursting through the clouds into the room. Abigail's hair glowed an unearthly white.

He watched her a moment, wishing she were here under different circumstances. Wishing he'd met her anywhere else—a bar, hell, even at one of Donner's charity events. He shook the bottle, effectively breaking the spell he felt himself falling under.

"Found some," he murmured. She swiped her cheeks as she turned to face him. So he pretended to ignore her tears, trying to give her the privacy she obviously craved. He had to get out…now. He wanted, needed something to ground himself in, but it couldn't be this woman. Not here, not under these circumstances.

"I'm downstairs if you need anything."

She nodded. He handed her the bottle, her fingertips accidentally brushing his.

"Thank you." Her voice was soft.

He quashed the urge to reach out to her. To hold her and tell her it would be okay.

"I—"

"Yes?" he asked.

She stared at him a long moment and something passed between them in the moonlight. She didn't say anything; she just stood, looking at him. He could have reached out to her then and had her. Taking her to the bed behind them would have been so easy and both of them could have forgotten about the hellacious day that had just passed… for a while. But that wouldn't have been fair. Not tonight. The day she'd had was the very reason he wouldn't do it.

He waited. Watched her and wished again he'd met her somewhere, anywhere else.

"Nothing. I'd better get to sleep," she murmured.

"I'll be back to check on you in a couple of hours."

He left before he could do or say anything crazy. That would only compound the disaster that this particular job had become. He couldn't exactly pinpont when it had gone off the rails. But…he now had a woman in his bedroom who was a principal asset. His boss was most likely crooked. Perhaps a murderer. Getting physically involved with Abigail Trevor would take it from disaster to Armageddon.

Even knowing that, he had a feeling that Armageddon was inevitable.

Now he knew where he'd gone off track. Their kiss in the kitchen of the hotel suite. That was where everything has slipped out of his control and this whole downhill slide had begun.

Could he stop it from rolling completely off the cliff? Could he just stay away?

Probably not. Biggest reason—he didn't want to.

That was the problem.

He flicked on the television trying to escape his dismal thoughts. A late edition of the news prattled away. Fire trucks and police cars filled the screen. He recognized

Jason's condo immediately. At first he thought it was only a report of the fire.

The reporter was speaking earnestly into the microphone as a shrouded gurney was wheeled down the steps.

"Firefighters made a grim discovery several hours after starting to fight the blaze. The body of a woman was discovered in the condo at the epicenter of the fire. She has been identified as Therese Mattagon."

A picture of an attractive woman who could have been anywhere between thirty-five and fifty-five years old depending on her plastic surgeon flashed on the screen.

"Police are searching for two individuals at the scene who are material witnesses and wanted for questioning. Abby Trevor and Shaun Logan."

Shaun heard Abigail gasp on the stairs behind him. "No. That's the woman from the bathroom at the restaurant."

Aww. Jesus. Despite his best efforts, Armageddon had begun.

Chapter Twelve

Shaun was riveted to the television. How had he missed a body in Jason's apartment? He hadn't searched the entire place; there hadn't been time before everything went haywire. But still, who was Therese Mattagon?

Abigail stood frozen on the stairs, her face as pale as the moonlight streaming in the windows.

"Good Lord, what happened in that condo after we left?" she whispered.

He went to her. "It could have happened before we got there. That's really the only way it could have happened."

"But why would she be at Jason's? I mean obviously she wanted the file but why would someone kill her? She didn't have it." Abigail shook her head.

"Maybe those men we ran into didn't know that," he suggested. "Maybe she beat them there and they thought she had the file. Maybe she fought back too hard."

He didn't say the worst of what he was thinking. Maybe Therese Mattagon wasn't dead before the fire. She could have just been tied up in a closet he hadn't checked. That thought would haunt him for a very long time.

He swallowed hard. "Let's think this through. She leaves you in the ladies' room and goes directly to Jason's to look for the file herself. If someone else was there, maybe watching the condo, waiting..."

"For me? Oh, no! They thought she was me and killed her instead?"

For Therese Mattagon's sake, he hoped they had at least knocked her out cold or, God forgive him, that she'd been killed before the fire. The horror of being awake and tied up in a closet and then dying of smoke inhalation was the stuff of nightmares.

He refocused on Abigail who now looked stricken. Even though he hadn't said it, she'd figured it out. "Oh, no. Maybe Therese Mattagon wasn't dead before the fire."

She took in a deep gulp of air. "I can't... That's too horrible to think about. I... Oh, God..." Her voice broke and she started to cry, sinking to the steps.

He reached out to grab her, wrapping her in his arms. As she held on to him, he fought against the very strong desire to bury his face in her hair. Instead he focused on talking to her softly, gently. Rubbing his hand up and down her back, as he'd do to soothe a troubled child.

"We don't know anything yet," he said. "That may not be what happened at all. I checked upstairs, not every closet, but it was very quiet in that condo. If she was conscious, I've got to think I would have heard something." He was trying to reassure himself as well as Abigail.

She burrowed deeper into his embrace and he struggled to keep it impersonal but there were some things he wasn't going to be able to hide much longer. Unfortunately his body didn't know that it wasn't supposed to be responding to the woman he'd been fantasizing about having sex with and who was now, finally, in his arms.

She took a steadying breath and the storm of tears seemed to pass. She needed comfort. Any second she was going to realize that wasn't exactly what he was offering. But disentangling himself wasn't an option at this point.

She sank further into his chest and stopped.

Right. That's exactly what she thought it was. He was that happy to see her. He waited for her to say something, to push him away. At the very least to step back, but she didn't.

She sighed and tilted her head up—the tears still wet on her cheek. "Do you want me?"

"I think it's obvious. More than is proper after the day you've had."

He started to back away himself but she held his arm and kept talking. "I don't believe Emily Post could possibly cover what's happened in the past twelve hours. What I really need is to forget about today. It's been horrid on every level. I want to lose myself in you. To forget." She looked up at him then, the intensity in her amber gaze taking him by surprise.

"You're serious," he whispered.

She didn't say anything. Instead, she stood on her tiptoes and tilted his head down so she could press her lips to his.

He could taste the toothpaste she'd used earlier that belonged to him. Smell the shampoo she'd borrowed from him, as well. Running his hands over her butt, he pulled her closer and parted her lips with his tongue. He kissed her so she'd have no doubt about him wanting her.

She pulled back to look him in the eye again. "Yes, I am serious. I don't want to dream about limos with shattered glass, or people holding guns on me in powder rooms or burning condos. And I especially don't want to dream about my brother. I just want to lose myself for a while."

In mindless sex were the unspoken words.

The part of his conscience he'd truly thought was buried

till he'd met this woman earlier today made him ask, "And tomorrow? You won't be sorry?"

"I don't know. I might be…but I'm a big girl. I can handle it."

And just like that he knew what he had to do. His body was going to hate him and Abigail was, too. But he wouldn't pile on morning-after regrets to the horrors of the day she'd just endured.

"Ah, well. You might be able to handle it, Abigail darling, but I'm not sure I can." He reached up, and though it absolutely destroyed him, he unclasped her arms from around his neck. "I just don't think that my heart could stand it."

She stood there with her mouth slightly agape, her lips forming a silent *Oh*.

He prattled on, filling the deathly silence, knowing he was going to have to push further for the reaction he needed. "Yeah. Sorry. I just don't think this is a good idea for tonight. I'm supposed to protect you, not screw you."

"Oh?" This time she said it aloud and in a tone that let him know he'd hit the mark. Her voice actually ratcheting up just a bit. She drew back and he saw fire in her eyes.

There now, that was exactly what she needed. As much as he hated it. Rage would keep her going far better than falling into bed with him. At least that's what he was going to tell himself tonight when he was trying to sleep on his sofa that really wasn't very comfortable at all.

"Well, I certainly wouldn't want to interfere with you doing your job," she said.

No danger of her rethinking this idea. He watched, as she wiped her face and gathered a cool cloak of anger about her, seemingly dismissing what had just happened between them like she had those scorching kisses in the hotel suite earlier.

"It'll be better this way." He patted her shoulder in a brotherly way, despite the fact he was feeling anything but brotherly. "You'll see. So tomorrow morning—" he began.

"Shouldn't we call the police?" she asked.

He cocked his head. "We can do that tonight if you want. But you know what they're going to say, don't you?"

"No. What?" Her voice was colder than an arctic wind.

"As a person of interest, you won't be able to leave town. Our trip to get the file will be postponed."

She glared at him, weighing her options, then glanced at the television. "My God, who *didn't* break into Jason's condo today?" She shook her head. "Why haven't the police called you or me on our cell phones? That EMT took your number."

"I may have transposed a number—or three."

"Just like you told them we were staying at a hotel in Arlington?"

"Something like that," he said.

"So if you hadn't turned on this newscast, we'd have no idea they were searching for us?"

"That's right."

"And there's no way they can prove whether we'd seen it or not?"

"Uh-huh."

"So we can just go along like we'd never heard about any of this?"

"Abigail Trevor, are you suggesting that we don't go to the police?"

She shook her head. "It's not like they've been a lot of help so far. And if what you say is true, now all they'll do is keep me from doing the one thing that might actually help catch my brother's killer. So yes, that's exactly what I'm suggesting."

He would take successes where he could get them at this point. "Right. So we won't call them. We'll leave in the morning like we never saw the news."

"What about your boss?" she asked.

"Donner? What about him?"

"Won't he wonder about all this? Why you aren't calling?"

And let that be a lesson to him. Don't count successes when the bigger challenge was just around the corner waiting to bite you in the ass.

Here it was. His moment of truth. He should just say it: I've already spoken to him. Donner called while you were in the shower. I think he may be trying to trace my calls.

But he didn't. Not after what he'd just done to her.

She'd leave his butt here in the morning and never look back if he admitted he'd talked to Donner less than ninety minutes after promising not to—no matter what his justification was for doing so. He had to lie to her, no matter what happened later. He couldn't let her go out on her own. She'd be in too much danger.

Plus he'd never see that file or the key code.

He took a deep breath. "Because talking to Donner is a deal breaker, right?"

"Absolutely. I thought I was real clear about that."

He smiled and nodded. "The topic's closed then. So what direction are we headed tomorrow? Are you at least going to tell me that much?"

She glared at him, obviously still mad over his rejection. He longed to run a hand down her face but that would completely undo the anger he'd stoked up here.

"South."

He nodded. "How far south?"

"Pack a bag."

"You telling me any more than that?"

She gave an unladylike snort. "I still don't know if I can trust you."

He waited. That was fair. He'd definitely yanked her chain tonight.

"We're going to Clarksdale, Mississippi—the town where I grew up."

She turned for the stairs and he watched her walk back up to his room. He would have to wake her every two hours but between all he'd just found out and thinking of her lying alone in his bed, he wasn't going to sleep much between now and then anyway.

He waited until he heard the door snap shut before pulling out his cell phone. It was time to call in some favors.

He hoped like hell that Harlan was home.

HARLAN JEFFRIES ANSWERED on the third ring.

"H?"

"Yeah."

"'Tis me. Shaun."

"How are you? I didn't recognize this number. What's going on?"

"Long story. Are you going to be home tomorrow night?" asked Shaun, glancing at the newscaster now muted in front of a large weather map.

"Sure."

"I need a favor. Can you meet me?"

"Of course. You know that. Anything," replied Harlan.

Shaun explained an abbreviated version of the Zip-Net issue and asked for his help in checking out Abigail's family home in Clarksdale.

"Where are you right now?" asked Harlan.

"At my house in Tyson's Corner. We'll be in Mississippi tomorrow night. It'll be late."

"No problem. But that's a long drive for one day. Have you seen the weather report?"

Shaun focused on the television to see computerized bolts of lightning and clouds covering the southeastern half of the map. "Yeah. It's on right now."

"Tomorrow is going to be ugly. Be careful, and call me when you know what time you'll be getting in. You're welcome to stay with us here in Starkville. Gina'd be glad to see you. We'll put you up."

"Thank you but no. I've got…problems. I won't bring them to your house."

"Shaun? After everything you did for Gina, Adam and me? Spiriting us out of Texas and letting us stay at your house when everyone and their dog was looking for us? You know we're here if you need anything."

Harlan was a friend who really cared and understood. One of the only people in his life who knew about the fiasco in Iraq with Gregor and Storm's Edge. Excepting Harlan, Shaun had acquaintances only. And there were parts of himself that he'd buried so deeply, he'd forgotten. Forgotten what it felt like to have a friend who knew all the dark places inside and still reached out.

"Right. I know. I just…I'll meet you. It'll probably be very late when I call, H."

"S'okay. Gina's not sleeping anyway. Baby's due any day now—she hasn't been able to get comfortable. I'll talk to you tomorrow."

Shaun hung up. Encouraged for the first time in a long time. Maybe, just maybe, this was going to be okay.

Chapter Thirteen

Day Two—Evening

Abby sat in the passenger seat trying to get comfortable. They'd been on the road for ten hours now and she needed to stop and stretch her legs. It had started raining cats and dogs as Shaun was changing a flat outside Blacksburg, Virginia. They'd been making horrible time ever since.

Clarksdale was still at least ten hours away, even if Shaun drove like a bat out of hell, which he wouldn't do because of the slick road conditions. They should probably just stop. She'd slept horribly the night before—staring at the ceiling after being woken every two hours by Shaun, then waiting for him to come back and do it again. To top if off, this day seemed never ending. She vacillated between fury and mortification.

In retrospect, asking him to take her to bed because she wanted to forget had been a wretched idea and not very flattering to either of them. She was overwhelmingly relieved that he'd turned her down—unable to imagine this interminable car ride after a pity screw.

Earlier she'd swallowed her anger and attempted conversation but he wasn't in a chatting mood. He'd completely shut her down when she'd asked him again about growing up in Ireland. He didn't want her help with driving, either.

Feeling raw and prickly herself, at the last stop for gas, she'd finally given up and bought a romance novel along with a tiny reading light in the Stop and Shop for something to keep her mind occupied. Still, she couldn't keep from glancing at his hands on the steering wheel as he drove. Remembering how those hands had felt on her neck and shoulders last night, she stole a glance at his legs encased in the dark denim jeans. She shook her head to erase the images that conjured up, choosing instead to bury her head in the book.

At ten-thirty they were pulling into another truck stop with an attached restaurant when she looked up from reading and realized they were no longer on I-40W.

"Where are we?" She turned to him on the seat. "Shouldn't we be headed to Memphis to get to Clarksdale?"

"Yes, but we're taking a detour first."

"Through Alabama?"

"Do you remember when I said if I couldn't keep you safe, all agreements were off in regard to who I asked for help?"

She nodded.

"I think we need someone watching our backs when we go look for the file."

She started to say something but when he turned to her and she saw the expression in his eyes, the protest died on her lips.

"I've got a friend who is going to help us. I can't look for the file and look out for you, too. Harlan and I were together in Iraq. I'd trust him with my life. He's trusted me with his and with his family's safety in the past. Harlan's going to come and help us when we go to Clarksdale."

"Why didn't you tell me about this earlier?" she asked.

"I didn't want to argue and I was worried you wouldn't like it."

"You're right, I don't like it."

"Abigail, my job has always depended on my understanding and accepting my own strengths and weaknesses. I can't protect you and do what has to be done if someone is following us. I don't know what is going on here with Therese Mattagon's and your brother's murders but it's obvious people are after you now. You need to understand and accept the implications of that."

She listened to the steady *swish swish* of the windshield wipers even though they were parked in front of the restaurant.

"I'm not going to argue with you, Shaun. I don't even know what town I'm in. I've nothing to my name here but a duffle bag of clothes that you bought for me at Walmart. I may be hardheaded but I'm not a fool."

"You're taking this better than I expected."

She shook her head. "Not really. I'm frustrated that you didn't trust me enough to tell me earlier. That's the reason I don't like this, but I do understand why you want help."

The wipers continued to beat against the windshield.

"Where does your friend live?" she asked.

"Starkville. The plan was to meet him there tonight and go on tomorrow to Clarksdale. But we've made bad time today with the weather. There's no way we'll get there before two or three a.m."

For the first time since she'd met him, he sounded tired. There was no way he'd slept last night, either. While she'd been struggling to fall back asleep after he'd woken her every two hours, she suspected he'd stayed up long after— watching over her. Plus he'd driven the entire way today in this unrelenting rain. As tired as she was, he had to be completely wiped. He wouldn't stop for himself, but she knew he'd do it for her. And she had a good idea of how to make that happen.

"I'm exhausted. Can we stop for the night here? Would your friend be okay with meeting us tomorrow in Clarksdale instead?"

He was staring straight ahead at an old phone booth in front of their car before he turned to her, pinning her with his gaze. She didn't back down.

He had to get some sleep and if convincing him that she needed to rest was the only way to make him stop, then so be it. She was still irritated at him for not telling her about his plan sooner, but she wasn't rash and it would be dangerous for him to keep driving as worn out as he was.

"How's your head?" His arm was stretched along the back of the seat and his fingertips brushed her shoulder. She struggled not to startle. His touch surprised her. So much so that she didn't think before answering.

"A little achy, that's all." She wasn't lying, she didn't feel bad, but she was weary. Did he know she was asking for him, more than for herself? It didn't matter as long as he agreed.

He rubbed her shoulder absently, his mind obviously somewhere else as he stared at the phone booth. "Okay. I'm beat, too. We'll find a hotel. But let's eat first."

THEY DASHED THROUGH THE RAIN together huddled under an umbrella that provided less than adequate protection. "It's a monsoon!" Abigail grabbed his arm for balance as they slipped and slid through the restaurant door, their shoes making squishy noises on the linoleum floor.

Shaun shook his head and droplets of water flew. "My Gran would have called this little sprinkle a 'soft old night' back home." He smiled faintly at the memory of his late grandmother as Abigail tried to brush the water from her clothing and shoes.

"Soft old night? It's raining like mad out there." But she was laughing as she said it.

He shrugged, returning a grin. "We're a hardy lot."

"Indeed." She made a beeline for the restroom. "I guess us Southern girls melt in this kind of precipitation. I'm hoping they have one of those auto hand dryers for my tennis shoes. I stepped in a huge puddle. Back in a minute," she called over her shoulder.

He waited till she was around the corner and felt his own smile fade. Did he have enough time to make a phone call to Donner? He looked down at his wet clothes.

It wouldn't be noticeable if he got any wetter. Besides this was going to be a short conversation. He didn't trust his boss. Donner had too many gadgets and tracking abilities at his command. Even though Shaun wasn't going to talk long enough to let him trace their location, Donner would still want to hear something. And Shaun still had to play along as if he was keeping Donner in the loop. If Shaun didn't call, Donner would get antsy. And an ansty Donner was not a good thing. The man tended to act impulsively.

He opened the umbrella and jogged back outside to the dilapidated phone booth, hoping the phone was still operational. The glass door was cracked and the dial tone was fuzzy but the phone itself worked and the roof wasn't leaking. All good signs.

Donner answered on the first ring. "Where in God's name are you?" he demanded in lieu of a greeting.

"On the road. In the rain. Somewhere between D.C. and Florida." Did Donner know he was lying? Shaun had no way of being sure.

"Where you headed?"

"She's not telling me. Just giving me directions as we

go. I'll keep you posted, but I wanted to check in. What's up with the police? Any word about the fire or the woman who died there—Therese Mattagon?"

"You and Abby Trevor are wanted for questioning about the fire."

"I know. I saw the news report last night before we left town. Who was that woman? She cornered Abigail in the bathroom at the hotel restaurant before we went to Jason's condo. I didn't find out till later."

Donner uttered a foul expletive. "She worked R & D for our competition. According to our preliminary research her background was quite similar to Jason's."

"Dig deeper," urged Shaun. "She carried a gun. I'd venture to say at least part of her background was quite different from Jason Trevor's. Find who hired her and you may find who killed your engineer." Shaun checked his watch and looked at the large plate glass restaurant window.

Was Abigail back from the restroom yet? It was time to hang up.

Donner was talking again. "Possibly. Or we may just find someone else trying to sink us. I'll check with my contacts."

"I've got to go. Remember, I told Abigail I wouldn't talk to you. This may be hard for you to believe, but she doesn't trust you."

"Hmm. Sounds like this could be interesting. Keep in touch."

"I've got to go, Donner."

"I know that but you just remember. I hired you to do a job. You're my 'fixer' and I expect you to deliver, no matter what."

"Right. I'm on it."

Chapter Fourteen

Shaun hung up the phone with a sick feeling in the pit of his stomach. How long had he been on the call? Could they have traced it? He didn't think so, but Donner had all kinds of new prototypes and products that weren't on the market yet. Good thing he'd disconnected the car's GPS.

Sprinting through the rain, he slid into a booth just as Abigail stepped out of the ladies' room. He couldn't look her in the eye. He knew he was screwing up by not telling her about Donner but he was too far down that road to admit it. Even though he wasn't telling Michael where they were, lying to Abigail was eating him up. When had that happened? Why couldn't he just tell her about talking to Donner?

The woman who brought their food was a talker and when Abigail asked if there were any bed-and-breakfasts or hotels in town, the waitress gave them the rundown and three phone numbers. The first two places were full thanks to some kind of local festival that was going on but with the third call, they got lucky. A last-minute cancellation due to the weather…but one room only.

Abigail put her hand over the cell phone and raised an eyebrow. "You okay with that?"

"Yeah. I'm so tired, I'm going to pass out once my head hits the pillow."

She moved her hand. "We'll take it."

He stared at her as she disconnected the call. "What?"

"You sure you're okay with sharing a room?" he asked.

"Why wouldn't I be? Last night I asked you to sleep with me, didn't I?" Her eyes never left his. "You don't snore, do you?"

It took him a moment to realize she was joking. He forced himself not to look away as he answered. "No. I've never been told I snore." He didn't add that might be because he rarely stayed with a woman long enough after they'd had sex for her to know if he snored or not.

"Great. Me neither. We'll be fine." She turned away to gather her purse, never acknowledging the gauntlet thrown down between them.

He swallowed hard. Last night it had taken all of his self-restraint to let her walk away after she'd asked him to make love with her. He wasn't going to kid himself that he could do that again.

Sitting beside her today in the car he'd been hyperaware of every movement, every sound she'd made. It had made him positively surly. Being so close to what he knew he shouldn't touch. Not talking to her hadn't helped as much as he would have thought.

The last thing he'd meant to do was be rude, but she'd kept asking questions, and then he couldn't seem to stop himself from snapping at her. What was it about this woman?

Before he had met Abigail, he'd always been able to stay in control, to bite his tongue if necessary and use his charm to get what he needed from people—to see the job done. But that ability to stay cool and unaffected seemed to have deserted him. A couple of hours ago she'd gotten so mad at him, she'd finally quit trying to talk and started to read; at least he'd been able to breathe a little easier.

But then he caught himself rubbing her shoulder when they stopped in front of this restaurant. It was a completely unconscious move. He was shocked at how easy it was to reach for her. He no longer trusted himself where she was concerned.

There better be a sofa in the room or he was going up in flames. No way could he sleep in the same bed with her and not touch her.

ABBY SURVEYED THE VICTORIAN bed-and-breakfast, complete with a porch swing. The innkeeper checking them in looked like a grandmother from a Norman Rockwell print. The living room was filled with doilies, lace and two couples having drinks watching a big screen TV. She wished she could enjoy this—the wood burning fireplace, the lovely oak paneling, the ambiance.

Normally she loved B and Bs but for all her nonchalance, she didn't want to share a room with Shaun. She reached for her duffle bag and his hand closed over hers at the same time. She jumped and almost yelped as she yanked her hand away.

He made her extremely nervous. Correction. She made herself nervous around him.

Why was she freaking out over the idea of sharing a room with him? It was crazy. He so obviously felt nothing toward her but "obligation." Of course, that thought was depressing as hell.

She tried to focus on the lovely surroundings while Shaun carried both bags up the large staircase to their sumptuously furnished room. Located at the end of a long hall, the Hawthorne Suite had a private bath with a tremendous claw-footed tub and shower combo containing exotic toiletries, plush towels and sweet-smelling candles. Nothing would feel as good as a long soak in that tub—after Shaun was dead asleep.

The bedroom itself held a cozy sitting area with a love seat, coffee table and overstuffed chair along with an antique armoire. There were luscious draperies covering the windows and a bed…the size of a postage stamp.

Actually it was a double. She desperately wished it was a queen or better yet a king, so there'd be no chance of her touching him accidentally in the night. She might spontaneously combust.

He shut the door and suddenly she was acutely aware of everything about him. How he filled the room. How his stillness made her conscious of every movement she made. As she watched, he seemed to unwind a bit. It struck her that in addition to everything else, he had been on hyperalert the entire day. Perhaps now he could relax, too.

Surely they were safe here. They'd paid in cash and he'd used a different name on the registry. It sounded like he might be going to sleep immediately. She sincerely hoped so.

"Do you want to grab a shower first?" she asked. "I'd like to take a long soak in that tub. I'm happy to wait."

He looked up from the small love seat he was staring at. His eyes were unreadable. "Sure, I'll be quick and you can soak away."

"That way you can go ahead and get to sleep. I don't want to keep you up."

"Right." He hustled into the bathroom, shutting the door rather firmly and thirty seconds later she heard water running.

As she unpacked her meager belongings, there was a knock on the door. It was the grandmotherly innkeeper with a carafe, a plate of fruit and chocolate.

"I brought you two some wine, a Shiraz. It's complimentary on check-in. After your long drive, I didn't know if you'd be coming down or not."

"Thank you, this is lovely," said Abby. "We appreciate it."

"You're welcome. I also wanted to let you know I just heard the weather report. It's going to get nasty tonight. Terrible thunderstorms and such. If we lose power, there are matches in that bedside table and you see the candles all around, of course." She pointed to various pillars and tapers throughout the room.

"Yes, thank you."

The elderly woman nodded. "Nothing like a booming thunderstorm for good sleeping. See you in the morning."

They'd made the right call in stopping. Driving in this weather would have been terrible. But no electricity, just candlelight? That would *not* calm her nerves.

She poured herself some wine. She could only hope Shaun was asleep before the lights went out.

The shower shut off and she gulped a large sip of the Shiraz before refilling her glass. On second thought, stopping here had been a terrible idea. Surely they could have driven farther.

Five minutes later Shaun stepped out in black knit basketball shorts and a tight fitting T-shirt. She struggled not to stare. How could she have ever thought this man was a software engineer?

He was so obviously…fit. His shoulders and thighs were huge. He looked bigger standing here in the romantic bedroom than he had anywhere else before now. She stuttered, explaining about the storm and the wine before finally escaping into the bathroom with her own full glass. The wind was moaning like a woman in labor when she emerged twenty-five minutes later and found him under the covers, his eyes closed. She wasn't sure he was really asleep but she was grateful he was pretending to be even if he wasn't.

The lights flickered once when she was in the tub and she had a feeling the electricity wasn't going to last much longer. Thunder crackled and her nerves zinged in time with each lightning flash. Putting off the inevitable, she poured the last of the wine, filling her glass again to the top. She noticed he'd had some, too, and she grabbed a chocolate as well, not caring that she'd brushed her teeth moments ago. She needed the comfort as well as the liquid courage before climbing into a bed that now appeared to be the size of a pool float.

Her Walmart pj's consisted of a cotton camisole and shorts and left her feeling overexposed. She hadn't been expecting to attend a pajama party when she'd selected them. Last night she'd been shopping for comfortable not concealing. But if she'd known about this, she'd have gone for the flannel granny gown.

To hell with Karen and her comment about "panty-melting" Irishmen. With what she *didn't* have on here, there was too much opportunity to bump into Shaun and all his lovely skin on that mattress that appeared to be shrinking by the second. Just thinking about it made her sweat.

She could blame the overheated feeling on the bath-water having been too warm, but she wasn't going to lie to herself. Ever since she'd kissed him in D.C., she'd been trying to avoid thinking about what it'd be like to sleep with Shaun. This was not exactly what she'd imagined. Still, crawling into bed with him was unavoidable at this point.

Taking another cleansing breath and a deeper sip of the wine, she turned toward the bed with the chocolate in her mouth. Thunder and lightning crashed together, shaking the windows. The lights flickered once…twice and went out for good.

"Well, hell," she muttered around the chocolate. "That's just perfect."

Chapter Fifteen

Immediately Shaun was up and moving, drawn toward her like a magnet. He'd done the best he could to give her some privacy when she came out of the bathroom, keeping his eyes closed and pretending to sleep even though he'd peeked just a little when she was roaming about the room. That hadn't been one of his better ideas.

Her barely there pajama shorts and top were now forever emblazoned on his brain along with her silky smooth legs. He'd been fantasizing about her body all day while she'd ridden beside him in that car. Now he didn't have to imagine anymore. To have her uncovered and exposed like this was a combination of torture and delight.

"You okay?" He walked toward her in the darkness.

"I'm fine. I…I can't see anything though. It's so dark."

"Right, just stand still. Your eyes will adjust in a few seconds." He was several feet from her at the end of the bed.

"I'm not scared but I am holding a very full glass of red wine and I'm going to spill it all over myself and the floor if I try to move." There was a tremor in her voice.

"Then don't." He was beside her now, gently touching her shoulder. He told himself that was to orient his body in the darkness but it was a lie. He wanted the excuse to touch her. Her skin was just as soft as he remembered from the neck rub and the night before. It took an effort not to stroke his hand across her back.

"Wine, we can take care of. Want to share?" he asked.

"That I can manage." Her arm accidentally brushed against his but he remained completely still.

Slowly he took the glass and drank deeply. Rain pelted the window with the curtains drawn loosely against the storm. He felt her straining to see him through the darkness. She was standing so close. Her body, still warm from the shower, threw off heat and smelled like flowers and chocolate. His own body responded and he took another sip of the Shiraz before wrapping her fingers around the goblet's crystal stem.

"Your turn." He moved his palm to her waist to steady her and heard a sharp intake of breath. He visualized her hands wrapped around him and worked not to tense his grip on her.

Lightning flashed outside and he caught a glimpse of her standing before him. Her head tilted back as she sipped the wine. So close. If they'd been lovers he would have leaned forward and kissed the hollow in her neck and worked his way downward from there.

"Were you asleep?" she asked.

"Not yet."

"All that thunder, I guess I'm not surprised." She took another sip. "Just a 'soft old night,' no?"

He could tell from her voice that she was smiling.

"Indeed. Some would call it that," he murmured. The moment stretched out. The sound of the rain surrounded them.

"I'm not sure I can drink all this," she finally said.

"That's because you're not sharing."

"You're right." She held out the crystal goblet and his fingers wrapped around hers again.

He didn't take the glass from her this time, instead he took her hand, still holding the goblet, to his mouth. He was torturing himself but he didn't care. He wanted her and this way he could look at her in the darkness and not have to hide what he was feeling.

He kept hold of her waist. If he took one more step, she'd be in his arms. Outside lightning slashed across the sky and thunder roared, shaking the windows again.

She shivered. He tightened his grip ever so slightly without pulling her to him.

"It's okay. You're safe here," he murmured.

He needed to stop touching her. But then she put her hand on his shoulder, steadying herself in the dark, drawing herself in.

Surprised he wasn't burning her with his stare, he drained the wine glass and reached around her to put it on the table behind them. Her breasts brushed his chest. An electric hum charged the air that had nothing to do with the storm outside.

"Do you want to go to sleep now?" he asked.

She didn't answer and for a moment he thought he'd finally spooked her. Then she rested her head on his chest and he was lost.

"No, that's not what I want." She tilted her head up and part of him wished for the lights to see her while the other part was grateful it was dark because he knew this wouldn't be happening if the lights were on. Darkness was making her braver than she would have been otherwise. What she would have seen in his face right now would have frightened both of them.

"I want you to take me to bed." Her words, spoken barely above a whisper, shocked him.

For a split second he wasn't sure he'd heard her correctly. Then she kissed the side of his neck and he didn't need any more encouragement as he ran a hand under her camisole, up her back and his other hand down her hip, pulling her into him so there was no doubt that he was completely on board with her idea.

"You're sure?" he asked.

She nodded and put her palms on his cheeks before pulling his face down to hers.

"Yes."

He kissed her then, tasting the Shiraz and chocolate on her tongue. She melted into him as he slid both his hands under the elastic of her pajama shorts and pulled her completely against his erection. Kissing his way down her neck and chest like he'd imagined earlier, he walked her backward toward the bed, his hands on her soft curvy ass.

When the mattress hit the back of her thighs, she landed on silky sheets and he caught himself before falling on top of her. She started to giggle and they both ended up laughing as they untangled themselves. Then she was helping him out of his shirt and his shorts while he pulled off her top and those barely there shorts he'd never gotten a real good look at.

His night vision was shot to hell with the flashes of lightning followed by pitch black, but he didn't need it as he forgot himself in her. She had her hands on the hard length of him and she was nipping at his lower lip. She began moving down his body in the dark. Tasting and touching him everywhere. "Abigail, what are you doing to me?" he murmured.

"Do I need to explain?" she asked and once more he could hear the smile in her voice.

The laugh rumbled in his chest. "No, it's just…you make

me forget…" But that wasn't it. She made him *hope* for the first time in such a long time. How had she done that?

She lay her head on his thigh waiting for him to finish the thought.

"That's a good thing, right?" She was touching him again and he was definitely losing his train of thought.

"Right…it's all good." He quit talking and put his hands in her hair as she took him away. Outside the rain fell and the thunder crashed but he no longer cared. It was just this room, this woman and the darkness.

ABBY WOKE WRAPPED IN SHAUN'S arms with her face tucked against his shoulder. Thunder rumbled in the distance and rain beat against the roof, though not as ferociously as it had earlier. She wasn't sure how long she'd slept but the lights were back on and the digital clock on the bedside table was blinking red at 12:00 a.m. Could be 2:00 a.m., could be 6:00 a.m. She had no idea. She started to raise her head but realized she would wake Shaun when she moved.

How had she ended up here? The last time she'd woken up in bed with a man had been over a year ago in Rome. She'd been leaving within a month, so the Italian history professor had been safe.

She looked down at the body of the man she was sprawled across. The sheet was bunched at his hips and she took the opportunity to study him like she hadn't been able to the night before.

Shaun was many things. But *safe* was not the first word that sprang to mind. His shoulders were impossibly broad and he had an intricate Celtic cross tattooed on his left biceps. The circular portion of the design was so detailed, it almost looked three dimensional even though everything was in black ink. Truly a work of art.

A wicked-looking star-shaped scar was at his waist. She leaned forward, ever so slightly. Was that a gunshot wound?

She stared at the uneven skin tone—obviously a severe injury—and wondered what had happened to him. She noted other marks, too. A jagged line ran along his shoulder and another mottled spot marked his collarbone. Aside from references to his grandmother, he'd avoided mentioning his past life, except that one veiled reference at dinner the first night and needing more wine to discuss it.

His words hadn't indicated an idyllic childhood. He'd only told her what he did now for Donner, and that he'd done the "same type" of work in the past, but these marks indicated something more than fixing DUI arrests and paying off mistresses.

Like perhaps a war wound? She examined the tattoo again and gently traced the scar at his side, re-evaluating what precious little he'd told her about himself.

He certainly hadn't minded her touching him there or anywhere else last night. Abby wasn't shy about her sexuality, still, Shaun was overwhelming in his intensity, plus he could switch it on and off with such control. The passion had seemingly come from out of nowhere. He'd turned her down cold at his home in Virginia and ignored her all day long in the car.

She'd have thought he was completely unaffected by her, even after their episode in the hotel suite, up until he inhaled her last night. She hadn't been able to read him beyond the overt physical reactions because it was dark. Then she hadn't cared anymore, staggered as she was by the power and desire he exerted—whispering to her in what she assumed was Gaelic while he made love to her with such ferocity.

But now she wondered. Before, he'd been so very private

with her. So closed and cool except for that one remark about his Gran and the weather. Charming, of course, but he could turn that charm on and off like a faucet—just like he could his physical reactions to her. And she was all too familiar with the secrets charm could hide. So far, he hadn't been willing to share anything of himself except his body.

That she understood. Failed relationships were her forte and she always made sure she had her own getaway built in. Her Italian history professor last year was a case in point.

She'd known all along she was coming back to the U.S. within six months so she'd had a natural escape hatch with her job assignment. Any relationship she started there couldn't be anything more than a short-term fling. In the end the professor had wanted her to consider staying in Europe but she'd refused. He'd been hurt, but she'd been unmoved.

She'd read enough to know her mother and father's horrific choices had a great deal to do with her approach to intimate relationships. But there came a point when you couldn't blame your parents or your past anymore for your present failures. She still couldn't figure out how she'd ended up making love with Shaun last night but she wasn't going to panic. This could still work.

He was protecting her until the threat was over, so it was only short-term. The trust issue here wasn't about anything intimate between them, even though the stakes were quite grave. The trust was about something much more basic. She just needed to quit thinking and she'd be fine.

She looked across his perfectly sculpted chest and decided she'd worry about her escape route later. Tiny crinkle lines were at the outer corners of his eyes and deeper laugh lines bracketed his mouth. She put her hand up to touch the faint scar under his chin. The one she'd noticed that first day in the limo when he'd been on top of her. She was bolder now that she'd been studying him for a while.

His mouth turned up at the corners and she drew back. "See anything you like?" he whispered, his voice wrapping around her like a warm blanket.

"You're awake."

He opened his eyes and grinned.

"Why didn't you say something?" she asked.

He sat up on an elbow and deliberately looked her up and down, scorching her with his Caribbean blue-green gaze. She pulled the sheet closer and willed herself not to scoot away in the bed.

"You seemed to be a lot more comfortable thinking I was asleep." He moved closer, reaching for her and leaving no doubt as to what he had in mind. "I assure you, I'm not sleeping."

"So I, um—" she laughed, her eyes darting downward for a moment "—see."

She went into his arms willingly. Unsure as to why she felt shy after last night except that she was thinking again and it was no longer dark.

He held her loosely in his arms. "You okay with this?"

Her head was once more against his chest—his heartbeat loud in her ear, the sound of it resonating in her own body, even over the rain. "I think so. Dunno, honestly. This is all happening so fast."

He pressed a kiss to the top of her head and pulled away from her slightly. "So…we'll slow it down a bit."

"Don't." She pulled back as well, propping herself up to stare into his face. "That's definitely not what I want." She levered herself on top of him and felt what was undeniably a sign that he did not want her stopping.

Then his hands were on her butt and she was kissing his

neck and working her way across his chest to a flat rounded nipple. She circled it with her tongue and heard his sharp hiss of breath when she nibbled at it with her teeth. "This is what I want," she said.

"Abigail…"

His voice was lost in the sounds of the storm outside.

"Shh…" she murmured. "I never thought I'd say this because I love to hear your accent but sometimes you talk too much."

He laughed and said nothing more as the storm played itself out.

Chapter Sixteen

Day Three—Late Morning

Shaun shut Abigail's car door with more force than necessary and made his way to the driver's side. If he could, he'd have kicked himself to the vehicle. How had he allowed this to happen?

Sleeping with her had been a huge mistake—an awesome, earthshaking, rock-his-world mistake he'd like to repeat as soon as possible.

He'd never had morning-after regrets, not because he hadn't slept around but because he'd always been careful about who he slept with. He avoided women he could see himself with beyond the short-term. His job and lifestyle were not conducive to long-term commitment.

That had all changed this morning when he woke up fantasizing about a life with Abigail after this was over. He had pillow shock for a completely different reason than the typical reaction to a one-night stand. Because when he'd been lying there, running his hand along Abigail's waist, still half-asleep, he'd started thinking maybe they could have a future together.

Maybe she'd want to be with him.

Maybe this relationship could be different.

Then he'd turned his head, spied his gun on the bedside table and reality had bitch slapped him in the face.

Abigail didn't want him. She needed his protection until this was over. Then she'd be gone. Especially when she discovered that he'd been talking to Donner since that first night, after she'd made him promise not to. He couldn't forget he had started this whole relationship based on lies. That wasn't likely to go over well when she found out.

Indeed. He was screwed—in every sense of the word.

So for now he had to get back to business.

He slammed his own door and the rich aroma of the B and B's gourmet ground coffee surrounded him. The innkeeper had fortified them with a hearty breakfast and "to go" cups before they'd checked out. He took a scorching sip of the brew to put off facing the inevitable.

Now that he'd slept with Abigail, his objectivity was out the window. There was no unringing that bell. He hadn't said much to her since they'd showered together in that massive claw-footed tub and he assumed she had to be confused since he was confusing the hell out of himself.

That was the problem to be addressed right now. He adjusted his seat belt and shoved his keys into the ignition. He only hoped their night together wouldn't make things awkward when they met the addition to their "field trip."

"Time to head out," he said.

"Yeah?" She turned from the window and smiled cautiously. "How about we go to Mexico instead of Mississippi?" She was a trouper, he'd give her that, trying to lighten his obviously bad mood.

He forced a smile himself. "Not today. But don't forget, we're meeting that friend of mine."

She stopped with her coffee in midsip. "That's right. I'd forgotten. Um…I'm not sure about this, Shaun. It makes me nervous."

He cleared his throat. "I understand your concern but believe me, you can trust him."

"No, *I* can't. *I* don't know him."

"Abigail, don't do this."

"Do what? Argue? Tell you the truth? Tell you how I feel about this, even though you're obviously holding things back from me and slamming doors and skulking about like a child?"

"No, just don't make this harder than it has to be."

She didn't answer but simply glared as they sat, still parked in front of the bed-and-breakfast.

"Do you trust me?" he asked.

"I don't know. You're making it difficult."

He laughed. "That's the smartest thing you've said to date. I'm not a safe bet."

"Yes, but I've already placed my bet, haven't I?" She didn't say it but the unspoken words were: *I did that last night.*

"Besides, it's more about trust right now than anything. It'd be easier for me to say I love you than I trust you," she continued.

He felt his face form a mask of disbelief. Then she laughed, but there was a trace of underlying bitterness in the sound.

"Don't worry, that's not what I'm saying," she explained. "I've always had a difficult time with trust. My parents said they'd love my brother and me no matter what. Unconditionally. But they didn't. When Jason told them that he was gay, they cut him out of their lives irrevocably. After all this time, I still can't believe they lied to us." She shook her head. "I've slept with you. That's as close to trust as I can give you."

He stared at her a moment. She'd told him about her parents at dinner two nights earlier and he'd known they'd left her with trust issues, but he hadn't realized they ran this deep. He'd made a serious miscalculation lying to her about his phone calls to Donner but he couldn't let her know. So he turned on the charm and smiled instead. "All right, Abigail, but please, don't sleep with Harlan. His wife wouldn't like it."

When she laughed, he heard the edge to it. He started the car and backed out of the B and B—a sense of dread spreading through his body. He got out of town and onto the highway as quickly as possible.

Could he tell her the truth now?

He glanced at her, trying to figure out how to start the conversation.

She was settling into the seat, tucking her legs underneath her butt. Her eyes were closed and she'd leaned back against the headrest. She was probably five minutes from being asleep.

He could do this. But how to explain?

He just had to say it:

I've been talking to Donner. I knew he would suspect we were up to something if I didn't stay in contact and I was worried he would send people after us to track us. This way we've stayed out in front of him.

That sounded reasonable. Hopefully it would work. At least it was a start. He considered pulling over but decided a high rate of speed was a better plan. She'd have to at least sit and listen to his whole explanation even if she was angry. He glanced her way, opened his mouth to speak and her phone started ringing.

Her eyes flew open and she fumbled in her bag to answer. "Karen? Hey, how you doing? Everything okay? No…no, calm down, I'm fine."

He tried to ignore the sense of relief he felt at having been spared his confession for the time being.

"Right. Well, no, I'm not in D.C. right now. We're going to my family's house. Yes, with him. It's…complicated. I'm okay. Please don't worry. I'm in good hands. No, I wouldn't go quite that far. Hmm…details, right."

Was she talking about him? He got a weird feeling in his gut as he listened to the one-sided conversation. His earlier relief was short-lived.

"Wait, Karen. Slow down. Who was there? What kind of questions were they asking?"

He sat up in his seat.

"Okay…no, you did exactly the right thing." She put her hand over the receiver to explain. "Someone's been at the facility asking questions about me and you." She went back to the phone conversation.

His mind raced. Someone had made contact and was asking Karen questions? It could have been Therese Mattagon's people or Donner's. Either way it was bad news.

"You know that's always been my biggest issue but I do believe he's…um…trustworthy in this sense."

He glanced at her phone and the uneasy feeling multiplied exponentially. She'd used Donner's phone in that hotel suite. His boss had practically insisted. That meant Donner could be using some new voice recognition software to keep a bead on Abigail, too. It didn't prove he was dirty, although that was most likely the case. At this point, there was no time to waste if they wanted to stay off his radar. If her cell phone was already on the grid, they'd be watching for any incoming or outgoing calls. Donner could be tracking as well as tapping her line through this call. The reason didn't matter.

He knew what he had to do. The one upside was even if he was wrong about the line tapping, he could solve multiple problems at once. Unfortunately, there was no time for explanations or charm. He reached for her cell phone, his hand closing over her fingers and the speaker. "Finish it now. I think that call can be traced."

Her eyes grew wide. "Karen, I've got to go. I'll get in touch when I can. Don't worry about me and don't call me back. I'll—"

He punched End.

"—call you." Her voice trailed off, her eyes wide with hurt and uncertainty. "Why did you do that? Karen will worry about me now."

"Why? Because every second you spent on the phone was time someone could have been tapping your line, knowing exactly what was being said, as well as tracing our precise location."

It took a moment for the implication to register. Her mouth opened in an understanding *oh*.

"Do we have any idea who was questioning Karen?" he asked.

She shook her head. "They showed up last night wanting to know if she'd heard from me. Asking if she knew you."

"What did she say?"

"She played dumb. Told them she'd talked to me the day of the funeral but that was all. Said she had no idea who you were. Do you really think Donner is tracing or tapping calls?"

He shrugged. "I don't know, honestly. I believe he's capable of it from a technical standpoint. If he is, it might just be because he can't stand to not know where we are and what we're doing. You met him, I'm sure you could tell that he doesn't like being left out of the show."

"And if you believe that…" She rolled her eyes and he glanced down at her phone, coming to a decision. If he hadn't been so worried for her, he would have been kinder.

"No more incoming or outgoing calls." Keeping his eyes on the road, he rolled down the window, slipped the battery off and tossed the lithium ion wafer.

He handed her the useless phone and she exploded. "Why did you do that?"

"No more temptation."

"I wouldn't have called anyone! All you had to do was trust me to turn it off."

He hesitated a moment before glancing her way and answering. "You just got through telling me that you weren't sure you trusted me. I can't take the risk right now."

The anger in her eyes told him that he'd solved more than one problem. She was cut off from everyone and everything she knew with the added bonus of being completely furious with him. She'd never let him close enough to get in her bed again.

Mission accomplished.

She was safe on all fronts. So why did he feel like a failure?

THE RAIN DID LITTLE to cool Abby's anger as they ran into the Burger King on Highway 61 in Clarksdale. Shaun had stopped at a pay phone and arranged to meet his friend there. He wasn't making any more calls on his cell, either. He had turned his off after tossing her battery out the car window. He and Abby had barely spoken in the six hours since. It was like last night had never happened. She knew she was going to have to be a lot more Zen about the situation but she wasn't there yet.

Still, her mother would have been proud of her manners as Shaun introduced her to Harlan Jeffries. She was polite and they grabbed a bite to eat while she got her first look at the man Shaun had called to help them.

He was huge, obviously from working out. He was taller

than Shaun and had a fishhook scar above his eyebrow that made him almost scary looking because of his size. He was wearing all black, including a baseball cap, and he would have appeared downright menacing if she hadn't seen the hat's embroidered multicolored ribbon divided into puzzle pieces with the stitched logo that read I love someone with Autism. It was difficult to be intimidated by him when he was wearing that cap.

Shaun asked after his wife, Gina, and their adopted son, Adam. When Harlan Jeffries smiled, she wondered why she'd ever thought the man scary at all. She ate her food trying not to be charmed by him and the familiar comfort of his Southern boy manners.

She excused herself to the ladies' room and when she returned they were deep in conversation. She didn't mean to eavesdrop but Harlan's words stopped her in her tracks.

"Did you ever have to testify?" he asked.

Shaun shook his head. "No. Gregor got himself killed before it ever went to trial."

"Well. That was good of him. The one decent thing he did," said Harlan.

Shaun stared at his unfinished burger. "Small favors, I suppose." He looked up and saw Abby standing there. She wasn't sure what she'd just heard but she knew it hadn't been intended for her ears.

"I'm sorry," she said. "I didn't mean to—" The words stuck in her throat. That wasn't true. Of course she'd meant to. She was desperate to know what Shaun was about.

Harlan glanced up at her but his eyes were kind. "Think I'll grab a refill and give Gina a call before we leave."

Harlan left Abby standing there and she watched him walk toward the counter. Sounds of the restaurant echoed around her. Children laughed. A baby cried. Workers bustled about behind the counter among various bells and timers going off.

She stared after Harlan a moment longer, tying to figure out how she'd ended up here alone with Shaun again. He so obviously didn't want to talk with her about this.

"I'm sorry—" she repeated.

He held up his hand to stop her from speaking. "You must be wondering. I worked for a civilian company that did security for contractors and troops in Iraq—Storm's Edge."

Abby couldn't prevent the sharp intake of breath. Everyone had heard of Storm's Edge. It had been all over the newspapers when the largest civilian security contractor in the Middle East had declared bankruptcy and ceased its operations overnight.

"I see you're familiar with the company. My boss, one of the founders, raped an Iraqi woman—a girl, really—and then tried to cover it up. It was ugly."

He took a sip of his soda before continuing. "When it happened, I tried to help her. Her parents didn't understand what was going on until it was too late. And that was a nightmare. I'm pretty sure the girl's entire family died in the process. Gregor tried to kill me in Iraq, too. He was back here about to be indicted on some other charges last year when he got himself killed."

"Oh, God," whispered Abby. "I heard about that. He died outside Murphy's Point on the river, didn't he?"

Shaun nodded. "I met Harlan in Iraq. He pulled me from the wreckage of what was apparently an IED explosion. I was on my way to report the rape incident to the military command when my SUV exploded."

He was rubbing his arm now. "I was never sure if it was an actual IED or a bomb in the car itself. Harlan got me to a hospital and—since he was military—to people who didn't fall under my boss's influence. Baghdad is an easy place to get yourself killed if someone wants you dead."

"What did you do?" she asked.

"I survived. Came back to the U.S. to heal." He looked up at her and his eyes broke her heart. He shrugged. "Apparently, a bit of a lost cause, that. Maybe I'm just a little too broken to put back together completely. I started doing private security work. That's how I met Donner."

No longer angry, she was starting to understand his frustration of trying to protect someone and not being able to do it.

"We've got a problem." Harlan hurried to the table, with a cell phone to his ear.

"What is it?" asked Shaun.

"Have y'all looked at the TV news lately?" asked Harlan.

"No," replied Abby.

"Not since the night before last," said Shaun. "The electricity went out at our bed-and-breakfast right after we checked in." He was so smooth, no one would ever guess what they'd done when the lights had gone out. Abby struggled to pull her attention back to the Burger King and the problem at hand.

"Gina tells me that you're both making your debuts in a big way on the national news." He slid into the booth beside Abby so they could be more discreet.

"What? I thought it would just be in the D.C. area," said Abby.

Harlan raised a shoulder. "You've graduated. You're wanted for questioning in the death of Therese Mattagon. Your pictures are being shown and there's a crawl across the bottom of the screen."

"But why? I don't understand," said Abby.

"We were in the condo the woman was pulled out of, so we're suspects," explained Shaun.

"What do we do? Call the police and explain?"

"I wouldn't advise that," said Harlan drily.

"It's almost six o'clock. I think we should head over to your folks' house and have a look before we run out of time and daylight here," said Shaun.

"You mean just ignore this?" asked Abby.

"For now," replied Shaun.

"But we can't take your car anymore," said Harlan. "I'm surprised you haven't been picked up yet in it. Let's take mine."

"Agreed," said Shaun. They grabbed their luggage and put everything in Harlan's Jeep.

Abby's childhood home was palatial by any standard and located about twenty minutes outside of Clarksdale. With Jason, it had been a magical place to grow up. But once her brother was gone, she had felt as if the walls were closing in on her. Today, she tried to remember the happier times without the bitter aftertaste—holidays around the Christmas tree in the living room, family games at the kitchen table, swimming in the backyard with friends from school. It was difficult to separate that ache of missing Jason from the good times they'd had together before he was banished.

The house was built in a Colonial Revival style—two stories, brick, shutters, columns, very spacious. Surrounded by cotton fields, it was set back from the road. The family farming the land had been doing so for years.

Since her parents' accident, the management company maintaining the property had been encouraging her and Jason to put their childhood home on the market. Even in this current economy, the area known as the original *birthplace of the blues* was growing. Year-round, Clarksdale hosted various music and arts festivals and people from all over the world passed through to see blues landmarks.

She and her brother had been putting off selling for various reasons—the biggest being they hadn't wanted to face going through all their parents' personal effects.

"I don't have a key with me to get in. We'll have to call the property management company," said Abby. "Let me get my purse. Their phone number is in my address book. I left in it the Jeep."

Shaun glanced at Harlan. "That won't be necessary," he said.

"Are you going to break in?"

"Technically, no. You're the owner and since you'll be standing right beside me when I open the door, it won't be breaking in. It will simply be getting you into a house that you are locked out of," explained Shaun.

She could see him skirting that gray area that she suspected he operated in a great deal of the time. They were on the front porch and Harlan was commenting on the massive oak trees in the driveway as Shaun knelt on one knee. She ignored them both and glanced at the empty brass mailbox beside the front door.

She wasn't sure exactly where to start looking for Jason's mysterious file. She supposed the kitchen. That was the last place they'd played dominoes together. Before she realized what he'd done, Shaun was swinging the massive front door open. She tried not to gasp but it was impossible.

Everything had been destroyed.

Chapter Seventeen

The house was completely trashed—recently, from the looks of it. Pictures were ripped from the walls, sofas gutted with stuffing and feathers from pillows littering the floor. Subflooring had been wrenched up in a few places as well and this was only in the living room just inside the entry.

Whoever had done this was obviously looking for something. Shaun immediately stepped in front of Abby and Harlan stood with his back to her, both acting as shields and pulling handguns. She hadn't realized either man was armed.

Slowly they made their way toward the back of the house where the destruction became more intense. Tables were overturned, mattresses shredded, even bathroom mirrors shattered. She could only assume whoever had done this had grown more frantic while making their search and coming up empty.

In the kitchen, a stainless faucet had been torn from the granite countertop. Several cabinet fronts had been ripped from the hinges. The destruction was as pointless as it was devastating.

A lifetime of memories was in tatters around them. Her life here may not have been idyllic but this had been her childhood home. Tears burned at the corners of her eyes.

She brushed them away in frustration and headed for the large table in the breakfast nook—the site of the dominoes game.

Deep gouges marred the surface of the burled wood—as if someone had taken a knife to the top in frustration. Her mother had loved this old antique. She'd purchased it at an auction when Abby and Jason were very young. They'd made tents out of it as children and lay on their backs staring at the underside—imagining themselves under the stars and hiding from Indians, in a mountain cave stealing dragon treasure and their favorite fantasy—in a castle living the life of a knight and princess. The tears stung and threatened to overflow as memories swamped her.

She realized she'd never told Shaun about what she'd seen in Jason's email video about being here, and it was past time she did. He and Harlan listened as she explained the particulars of why this table would be significant. Both nodded when she was done.

"But it's bothered me since I first saw the video clip. If Jason only sent the file and key code the morning of his death, how could they be inside the house? He wasn't here that day to hide them himself, and he didn't have time to do anything from long distance. The only places a package could have been delivered to were the mailbox or the front porch with UPS type deliveries. I don't think anything like that came. If the people who did all this found a package, why trash the house?"

She shook her head in defeat—her brother's words running through her head.

You were always so good at imagining things and you always were a helluva domino player. Remember the last time we talked about this?

In a last-ditch effort, she got down on her knees and lay on her back looking at the bottom of the table. Nothing was there but the underside of a ninety-year-old antique with the stamp of the furniture maker on it.

Faulkner Fine Furniture.

Faulkner. Faulkner.

William Faulkner had been the subject of Abby's thesis. Karen had been her college advisor for her thesis…*the last time we talked about this…*

"Oh, God," said Abby. *Karen?*

"What is it?" asked Shaun.

Abby almost banged her head getting out from under the table but she didn't answer. Instead, she sat in one of the dining chairs and stared at the marred top.

Karen had been at her parents' funeral. She'd been sitting at this table afterward talking with Jason. Had they mentioned dominoes? Abby honestly couldn't remember.

She had been too tired, too angry and too sad to focus that particular day. But her brother and Karen had talked and talked and talked about all sorts of things. The good memories he'd had about growing up in this house.

They must have talked dominoes at some point. Abby did remember Jason talking to Karen about lying underneath this table and their silly childhood imaginary stories.

God, she'd been slow.

Could he have sent the information to Karen in Dallas?

Abby only hoped she wasn't too late.

Shaun turned her to face him, a question in his eyes.

"Abigail, what is it?" he asked.

"The upgrade file and key code are in Dallas."

"You sound pretty sure."

"I'm positive." She explained to both men why she thought Jason had mailed everything to Karen.

"There's only one way to know for certain," said Shaun. "Do you have Karen's number memorized?"

She glared, the memory of her tossed battery still raw. "As a matter of fact, I do."

"H, can she use your phone? I'm concerned that ours can be tapped when we make calls."

Harlan raised an eyebrow but handed his cell phone over.

Shaun grimaced. "Okay, yes. Calls from your line can eventually be traced and tapped, as well. But your number isn't on anyone's radar yet, so using it will slow down any tracking considerably."

"Who's doing it?" asked Harlan.

"Jury's still out on that."

"Humpf," groused Abby.

"Put your friend on speaker," suggested Shaun.

Karen answered on the second ring. Abby didn't even get to ask the question before Karen interrupted her. "I've been trying to reach you for a couple of hours. I know you told me not to call but I've gotten some kind of package from Jason. It was mailed the day he died and got held up at the reception desk here because it needed a signature. I have no idea what this is but I definitely think you should have it."

A frisson of excitement and concern danced along Abby's spine. "Karen, does anyone else there know who the package was from?"

"I'm not sure. There's only a return address. No name. The FedEx sat at the desk downstairs for several days then at the nurse's station on the floor here for a few hours. If anyone was curious, I can assume they know *where* it came from but not necessarily from *whom*."

Shaun reached out and muted the phone. "Ask her not

to tell anyone else about it. Tell her that we'll be there as soon as we can but it will probably be tomorrow."

She nodded.

"How long would it take us to drive from here to Dallas?" asked Shaun.

"Seven to nine hours," said Harlan. "Depends on how fast you drive." He paused for a moment. "It'll take you seven." He grinned.

"We'll have to get another car before we can go," said Shaun.

"Take mine," said Harlan

Shaun was shaking his head. "I can't do that."

"Sure you can. What else are you gonna do?" asked Harlan.

"Hey, can you guys argue about this in a minute?" The two men swung back to face her. Abby still had the phone muted but to her ear. "Look, I'm glad to tell her I'm coming, but I can't scare her. She's had a stroke."

"Abigail, what do you think these people would do to Karen for that package?" Shaun asked, pinning her with his intense stare. The truth was frightening to face and she looked away to Harlan who nodded sadly.

"They'd...they'd kill her," she said.

"So scaring her just a little isn't such a bad thing, if it'll keep her safe, is it?"

She shook her head.

Karen was talking, too. "Abby, what's going on? Are you in trouble?"

"No. I'm fine, Karen." Her conscience only zinged her slightly for lying and she told herself it was for Karen's own good. "I'm sorry I can't explain over the phone but I'm coming to see you right now and I'll tell you everything then. I promise."

"Do you have your Irishman with you?"

Abby glanced up at Shaun and felt the blush bloom across her cheekbones. "He's right here."

"Good. Don't you do this by yourself."

"Yes, ma'am. See you in a few hours." She hung up and looked at Shaun and Harlan together. "So, we're going to Dallas."

Shaun nodded. "We are but Harlan's not. We're dropping him at a car rental place on the way."

Harlan cheerfully slapped him on the back. "Hey, buddy, standing right here. Am I suddenly invisible?"

"Not hardly," said Shaun, but he was laughing as he said it.

"How 'bout I come with you? How do you know these guys aren't on their way to Dallas, too?" asked Harlan.

"We don't," replied Shaun. "But you've got a very pregnant wife and I'm not taking you eight hours away from her this close to her due date. Gina would have my head on a stick."

"No, she wouldn't."

Shaun chuckled. "Never underestimate the power of a pregnant, hormonal woman, Harlan. I can't believe you haven't figured that out yet."

"Gina's not that way."

"Maybe not, but I'm still not doing it. I want to be invited to dinner when I come to town," said Shaun.

Abby smiled. "I see you haven't crossed her yet when she's been having a chocolate craving."

Harlan grinned. "Well, hell, any idiot knows not to do that."

"You'd be surprised." She laughed and it felt good.

They were headed for the front door, Harlan in the lead, his hand on the knob.

There was no warning. The front door simply imploded inward. Abby was knocked flat as Harlan flew backward, his head hitting the foyer wall with a hollow sounding thud. Shaun fell on top of her as flames burst from the kitchen behind them. Shaun was sitting up before she realized what had occurred.

Harlan wasn't moving; a trickle of blood oozed from his forehead. Flames raced along the ceiling. It was happening so fast. The air was on fire. This was Jason's condo all over again. A bizarre sense of déjà vu overwhelmed her.

"You okay?" Shaun asked, running his hands down her arms.

She nodded, still shaken, and glanced over at Harlan. "I'm fine. Check on him." Shaun's friend was too still and his arm was twisted at a funny angle.

He nodded and moved to Harlan, looking him over as Abby tried to stand up. "What happened?" she asked, still trying to clear the fog from her head. Everything was so loud.

"I don't know. Gas leak, maybe," yelled Shaun. "We've got to get out of here." He pulled her to her feet, pushing her toward the opening that had been the front door, then turned for Harlan. She struggled over flaming debris around the threshold and looked back. Shaun had Harlan in a fireman's hold, hauling him out behind her.

She'd made it to the first step on the porch when fragments of brick exploded around her. It took a moment to recognize what she was hearing over the sounds of the fire. More shards of brick flew up beside her.

Gunshots!

She looked up but couldn't see anything in the darkness. Her eyes were still adjusting from the light of the fire behind her. She headed back up the steps meeting Shaun along the way.

"Someone's shooting at us!" she shouted.

Chapter Eighteen

Shaun didn't hesitate. Still holding Harlan, he turned and headed back into the inferno. They raced through the living room, dodging flaming debris along the way. Smoke thickened the air. Abby could feel the pressure of it forcing the oxygen from her lungs. She was going to start wheezing any second.

The carnage from the break-in—flipped tables, chairs, lamps, torn books, magazines and pillows—coupled with the destruction from the explosion made it difficult to get past. The electricity was out but orange flames lit the way.

"If they're waiting at the front door, they may be waiting at the back door, too," said Shaun.

"What do we do?" she asked through her coughs. Smoke was growing thicker by the second. She dropped to her knees seeking clearer air, but it was useless. Her eyes burned and watered as her throat began to close.

"Is there a window?" he asked.

No longer wasting oxygen on speaking, she nodded, heading for the floor-to-ceiling casement behind an overturned sofa.

"Get down as you open it," directed Shaun.

Abby nodded again. Using the couch as a shield, she unlocked the window and pushed it open from a squatting

position. For a moment, bilious smoke poured forth and the
flames gusted toward the night air, seeking more oxygen
for fuel. Then she was falling into the Indian Hawthorne
bushes and Shaun was right behind her, lowering Harlan's
body into the branches. They lay in the landscaping for
a moment, gulping clean air and waiting to see if more
gunshots were forthcoming.

She was sweating and heard a slight whistling in her
own breathing. Willing the imminent asthma attack to hold
off, she crawled forward as Shaun pulled Harlan along
under cover of darkness. Seconds later they were in another clump of bushes fifteen yards away watching two
men silhouetted in the flames. A third joined them and
together the three circled the house, walking toward the
back. Shaun had been right.

"We need Harlan's keys," he whispered. "They're in one
of his pockets. Find them and we can get out of here."

"Okay." With a silent apology to his wife whom she
hadn't yet met, Abby started dipping into Harlan's front
jeans pockets as Shaun searched through his jacket. On
her second foray into his Levi's, her fingers closed around
a key chain. Harlan's eyelids fluttered.

"Gina?" he murmured.

"Nope, just me," she muttered under her breath. "Got
'em," she wheezed aloud.

"Great." Shaun pulled Harlan to his feet and half carried
half dragged him to the Jeep. A blue sedan was parked
beside it.

No doubt about it, she was having another full-blown
asthma attack now. It was like trying to suck in air through
a coffee stirrer. At the Jeep, Shaun was shoving Harlan in
with the obvious intent for her to drive since she knew how
to get to the E.R.

She'd barely shoved the keys into the ignition when

her hands quit working. "Gotta have meds," she managed between labored breaths.

Shaun stopped at the sound of her voice, recognizing what was going on. "Where are they?" he asked.

"Duffel…bag."

He didn't comment on her not carrying the rescue inhaler on her person. He just rustled around in the back of the car for fifteen seconds and came up with her medication, steering her to sit in the passenger seat as he shoved the plastic case in her hands.

She puffed on the inhaler as her butt eased back into the bucket seat. He stared into her face for five full seconds and without a word, left her to dash around the blue sedan beside them. She couldn't see what he was doing as he bent down beside the tires. She wasn't sure she wanted to.

She tried to relax, to concentrate on breathing through her nose and letting the meds do their thing. But watching her childhood home burn and "relaxing" were mutually exclusive.

No sirens sounded in the distance. It was too late for that, anyway. It had been too late from the beginning. The house was a lost cause.

She turned to look at Harlan, wondering if she should climb in back with him. His face was so pale but his chest rose and fell at a steady rate. His eyes fluttered once more. "Gina," he murmured again.

"It's okay, Harlan. Hang on."

Come on, Shaun, we've got to go. Those men would be coming back to the front of the house any moment.

Harlan was thrashing around in the backseat. His eyes were open now. "Jeez. What happened?" he asked.

"House blew. You got…whacked…in…head." Speaking wasn't any easier yet, but she was getting more air. The one positive in all this.

SHAUN LEAPED INTO THE DRIVER'S seat, shoving a pocket knife into his back pocket. "We're gone."

He cranked the engine and floored it, his heart racing as he studied the side mirrors. He'd cut it very close on time.

"What did you do?" she asked.

He was quiet, speeding down the drive and switching his gaze between the road in front of him, the rearview mirror beside him and the burning house. The three men were running toward them, but they were too far away to shoot…he hoped.

He stared out the back a bit longer.

"Shaun?"

He turned to her, shaken from his reverie. "I slowed them down. Slashed their tires. That'll give us a head start."

Her eyes widened and Shaun glanced back at Harlan. "Hey, H, welcome back. How's your head?"

"Hurts like hell, so does my arm."

"You took quite a hit. Your arm may be broken."

"We're taking him to the hospital, right?" asked Abby.

"Right," said Shaun.

"Wrong," said Harlan at the same time.

"You need to get checked out," argued Shaun. "You can call Gina from there to come get you."

"No," said Harlan through gritted teeth.

"Come on, Harlan, you're killing me here."

"What? Are you crazy? That'll scare Gina to death. No way."

"I'll call her myself if you don't go. You got thrown against a wall and you passed out. You go to the E.R. No arguing. Come on, man, don't be stubborn about this. You've had head injuries before. Besides, it helps us with the whole getting-to-Dallas-quicker issue, if you want to be pragmatic about it. I don't have to worry about how to get you home while I'm taking your car. You're getting what you wanted after all. Let's report it stolen now so you and Gina are completely out of this."

"Well, when you put it like that," Harlan relented just as Shaun knew he would. Keeping his family safe trumped everything—as well it should.

"Don't forget to swap out the license plates though," reminded Harlan. "Any big shopping center parking lot is a good spot for it, in case you're wondering. Look for one on the way to the E.R."

Shaun laughed. "Thanks for the tip, Clyde Barrow."

"I've learned a few things. It'd be bad if Clarksdale's finest picked you up before you got out of town."

"Won't they…find…yours and Harlan's connection?" asked Abby, still struggling for air.

"Yeah, but not right away. They'll be more focused on the stolen vehicle report than our association," explained Harlan.

It was much easier to do the swap than Shaun expected. They simply sat in a grocery store parking lot and watched someone deposit their car in a far corner. Shaun walked over and did the deed in less than five minutes. Thanks to Harlan's tool kit in the back of the Jeep, they were in the parking lot less than ten minutes. Harlan could now report his vehicle as stolen and get his family separated from this mess as quickly as possible.

Shaun climbed back in the car and turned to his friend. "You happy?"

"Ecstatic. Um… One more thing. I'm not calling Gina till after I'm checked out of the E.R.," Harlan said.

Shaun's blood turned icy. "No, I can't just leave you. I won't do that."

"Don't worry about it. You're dropping me and I'm

calling Gina after I check out. I'll tell the E.R. folks I fell off a ladder and a buddy gave me a ride. It's easy."

Shaun felt slightly nauseated. "You know why I don't want to do this."

"Yeah, I know and there's nothing to be done for it," argued Harlan. "I can take care of myself. I'm a grown man, not a teenage girl. You're not deserting me or letting me down. Don't worry." They were five minutes from the E.R. entrance, but Shaun and Abby couldn't risk either of them being seen in public with their pictures everywhere.

"You're sure?" Shaun asked.

"Yes," said Harlan. "We just went to a lot of trouble to sever my association from you. I mean this in the nicest way possible but I don't want you near me right now, okay? Besides, words a pregnant woman does not need to hear are *I'm fine but I'm on my way to the E.R.* She'll still be upset but much safer with *Come get me, baby. I'm okay. I just checked out of the E.R.*"

"I see your point," said Shaun. As much as he hated this, it couldn't be helped.

"If she's pissed, I'd rather have her pissed and driving the speed limit. And you," Harlan said, addressing Abigail and him, "are invited to dinner anytime. I'll be more than happy to see you when this is over."

Swallowing his unhappiness with the situation, Shaun smiled. "Ah, now. Don't be saying that 'less you mean it. You know I'll be taking you up on one of Gina's home-cooked meals."

He parked in the E.R. entrance where he hoped he was not in security camera range and got out to watch as Harlan spoke earnestly to Abigail. He couldn't hear a word through the window. He guessed they were talking about him if her gaze on him was any indication. Shaun opened the back door in time to hear Harlan say, "Believe me."

Abigail looked serious and so did Harlan. Lightening the mood was definitely in order. "Believe you?" joked Shaun. "Why, you're the most well-practiced liar I know, Harlan. And I have the poker stories and empty wallet to prove it."

Harlan looked up and grinned, cradling his arm. "No worries. I just told her that you believed in leprechauns and the fae."

Shaun smiled. "Of course I do. Always have. Can you get inside?"

Harlan stood and hissed in a deep breath as he jostled that injured arm. "I can manage. Trust me."

Shaun cocked an eyebrow. "On this one point, I don't. But I'm going to have to, aren't I?"

Harlan was turning back to Abigail when Shaun overheard something he knew wasn't intended for him. "Remember what I told you," said Harlan. "He's a good man. The best. He'll take care of you." Harlan clasped her hand before limping over to the curb.

Inwardly Shaun cringed. He knew he wasn't a good man. Not really—"well-practiced liar" was the more apt description. Harlan didn't know that Shaun had been lying to Abigail basically since he'd met her. He wondered what else Harlan had said about him, but he didn't have time to go into it out here it the open.

"I'll be in touch about the car. Thank you for everything, H. I don't know how to begin to repay you."

Harlan shook his head. "There's no need. You know that."

Shaun couldn't shake Harlan's hand because that was the arm that was broken. Instead he patted Harlan on the opposite shoulder and watched him do an awkward hobble-shuffle through the E.R. entrance. He didn't have another friend like Harlan. Shaun only hoped Gina would forgive him for putting her husband at risk, then leaving him here in the hospital alone. He waited till the sliding doors closed and Harlan disappeared into the building before getting back into the Jeep.

Shaun now had a whole new host of problems.

Abigail's asthma, for starters. Was he making a huge mistake in not leaving her at the E.R., too?

An hour ago he would have taken her in to be seen there before going on, but now he couldn't. That option was entirely too dangerous. It didn't matter what Abigail thought of him or Harlan or what he even thought of himself. He was the only one who could keep her safe.

That was the truth he had to concentrate on.

Everything had changed when he'd seen who was racing across the lawn with guns blazing at her parents' house. It had been a shock, especially as he'd worked side by side with the man before.

Donner wasn't just tracking him and Abigail as Shaun had feared. One of his security detail was trying to kill the two of them.

Chapter Nineteen

What was Hodges doing here trying to kill them?

It didn't make sense.

Shaun wasn't surprised that the man had found them. He'd known in his gut since their conversation after the condo fire that Donner was dirty. He just hadn't fully embraced it then. Hadn't wanted to believe he could be so wrong about everything…again. Wrong like he was in Iraq with Storm's Edge and Gregor. But there was no denying it now.

Shaun had seen the solid proof in his rearview mirror less than an hour ago. It had been Hodges racing after them. Shooting at them. Hodges, who was part of Donner's security detail. Hodges, who'd had military training as a sniper.

Christ. Had Hodges actually been the one shooting at Abigail in the cemetery?

There was no denying Donner was responsible for all of this. Hodges wouldn't be taking orders from anyone but him. And Shaun knew now that Hodges had been the one holding the gun in Jason's condo, too. Shaun had thought the voice sounded familiar. Hodges had probably even taken care of Therese Mattagon—though for the life of him, Shaun had no idea why.

It wasn't logical. With Jason dead and the file missing,

the sale to Homeland Security couldn't go through. The backups and bugs Jason had originally gone in to update and repair weren't fixed yet and now that Zip Technologies was locked out of Zip-Net? Donner had to have Jason's key code or the entire program was worthless. Abigail was their only link. Donner couldn't kill her before getting the file. The bigger question was: Why had they killed Jason to begin with, without that key code for the spyware?

Unless, they'd killed him before they knew he'd locked them out of Zip-Net.

That was the only thing that made sense.

Jason had found the spyware issue in the morning, locked down Zip-Net, emailed Abigail and overnighted the key code information and the upgrade file to Karen Weathers, then got himself killed on his way to tell Donner all about it.

Jason must have unknowingly talked to a colleague who was in on the scheme before he met with Donner—or he could have mentioned it to Donner on the phone when they set up their lunch appointment that day. The lunch appointment Jason never got to. Donner must have had apoplexy when he realized Jason had essentially locked them out of the kingdom and thrown away the key.

But where did Therese Mattagon come in? She had only threatened Abigail about the original updates. Most likely she had been spying on Jason before his death and just switched to Abigail afterward—looking for that upgrade file to block the sale and Zip-Net's success. Therese was part of the cutthroat competition.

But why kill her in Jason's apartment—unless Donner wanted to keep Abigail from going to the police? He'd known Shaun would discourage her from seeking out the authorities. And Shaun had played right into it. After the condo fire, it had been easy to frame them for Therese's death.

In Donner eyes, it had been a win-win situation. Framing Abigail and Shaun kept them dependent on him, reporting to him. Or if they chose to strike out on their own, Donner had all kinds of means to help the police catch them.

He glanced at Abigail. He had to tell her. She'd been right. Donner was rotten to the core, planning to screw Homeland Security with spyware in their new wireless system so he could sell classified information to the highest bidder once he got his hands on that key code and Jason's file.

Shaun drove on, knowing he had to tell her about this latest twist. Dreading what she was going to say. Her worst suspicions confirmed. Would she believe he'd been trying to tell to her for at least twenty-four hours that he believed the same thing?

He'd been so wrong not to confess to the earlier on-going conversations with Donner. Now there was no way to convince her that he hadn't been lying about everything, especially once he'd slept with her.

How had he made such a mess of this?

"Abigail, there's something we've got to talk about."

"Yeah?"

"Back there. One of those men at your house. I recognized him from Zip Tech. He works there." He glanced at her, saw how pale she'd gone and he murmured words he hadn't used in front of a woman in a very long time.

She completely surprised him by laughing out loud. "You know I was starting to wonder if you ever cursed. I mean serious sailor kind of cussing."

"Much to my grandmother's chagrin. She claimed I turned her hair gray when I was younger. I try to restrain myself now."

She nodded. "Your Gran sounds like a pistol."

"She was. I liked that about her, when she wasn't washing my mouth out with soap."

She laughed once more. "I would have paid to have seen that."

"She would have enjoyed knowing you." He looked her way again. The color in her cheeks was coming back. He forced himself to go on—hating to break the lighter mood, hating what he had to tell her next.

"The man I saw. 'Tis worse. He works—worked—for me on Donner's security detail."

She didn't reply at first but stared out the window into the night. Finally she asked, "So are you convinced now that Donner is responsible for Jason's death?"

He drove on. Knowing what he needed to tell her but unable to make himself say it all...so he compromised. In the interest of keeping her safe. She'd leave him if she knew the truth and that wasn't a safe alternative.

"Yes, I think it's true. I didn't want to believe it, but I do now. I'm sorry."

"You're sure?"

He could only nod. He couldn't force himself to speak the rest of it. The truth. So he lied by omission. *I know because I've been talking to him almost every day since we left D.C., and everything he's said has made my suspicions grow.*

She'd leave him if he told her that, and Donner's men would kill her. Once he had the upgrade file and key code safely in the hands of the proper authorities, she'd be safe and of no further interest to Donner.

So he was going to lie just a little longer, even as it took a bit of his soul to do it. Lying hadn't bothered him at all in the past. Now it made him feel like hell.

Once she found out he'd deceived her—and she was

going to, that was inevitable—their short-term relationship would be over. So not coming clean right away had at least one thing going for it: he could be with her till she found out the truth and told him to drop dead.

Day Three—Late Evening

"WHAT THE HELL HAPPENED?" demanded Donner. He punched the accelerator on his Porsche, speeding along the Parkway to the airport and his private jet.

"We lost them, sir." Hodges's voice trembled.

"You what?"

"We lost them," the younger man repeated.

"Let me get this straight. You had the house surrounded with three armed men. You blew it up with the woman and Logan inside after I expressly said I wanted them alive, and then you lost them?"

"Yes, sir."

"How long ago did this happen?" demanded Donner.

"Three hours."

"How in God's name did they get a three-hour head start on you?"

"Logan disabled our vehicle and there's sketchy cell coverage out here. We're walking to town."

Donner said something foul and scathing before taking a deep breath. "The irony of that statement is not lost on me, Hodges. Nevertheless I must have the updates and that damn key or this entire sale is lost. At midnight tomorrow we're supposed to turn over complete control to the Department of Homeland Security and right now we can't even turn Zip-Net on, much less get our window inside."

"Give me another chance, sir. We know where they're going." His voice was particularly deferential. Donner liked that in his employees.

"Why should I do that? You've screwed up multiple aspects of this job already. We won't even talk about what happened to Jason Trevor in Dupont Circle."

"An unfortunate miscommunication, sir. I did not receive the text to abort until after I'd completed the job."

"Hodges, a miscommunication is ordering anchovies on my pizza when I ask for pepperoni. Killing someone before I have a chance to ascertain if they have relevant information is not a friggin' miscommunication." He slowed as he approached the airport entrance.

"Yes, sir."

Donner sighed. Hodges was an idiot and a suck-up but he was loyal. Certainly more so than Shaun Logan. Besides, Donner was out of options until his plane landed.

"Don't misunderstand me. I want that upgrade file and the key code. I don't know for certain if the woman in Dallas has them, but all indications are she has something of value from Jason Trevor. He sent something to her the day he died. We just got the info from our corporate FedEx account this afternoon. So we'll start with Karen Weathers. If nothing else, she can be leverage, if those pictures we found in Therese Mattagon's briefcase are any indication."

Therese Mattagon had been the one aspect of this matter that had gone precisely as planned. Mattagon's corporate spying had put her in exactly the wrong place at exactly the right time to suit Donner's needs. Her death had served multiple purposes, including keeping Shaun and Abby off balance and looking to Donner for information as the police zeroed in on them as suspects in her death. In addition, Mattagon left a briefcase that held invaluable information on Abby's family background, some of which Donner had never seen before, even though he'd employed her brother for several years.

Hodges cleared his throat. "I'm on it, sir."

"Excellent. Don't screw up this time."

SHAUN AND ABBY DROVE ALL night, arriving in Dallas as the sun's rays peeked over the gold-mirrored buildings on Central Expressway. Abby yawned when they pulled into a Starbucks in a strip shopping center off Mockingbird Lane.

"Do you want to grab some coffee and something to eat before we see your friend or go straight to the rehab facility?" asked Shaun.

"It's not even seven o'clock yet. I hate to wake her up. Let's eat fast and grab something for her too, perhaps? She likes banana nut anything from here."

The temperature had dropped unexpectedly and the gauge in the Jeep read forty degrees. Typical for Texas in April. It could be eighty degrees one day and forty the next. Abby was shivering by the time they got into the coffee shop and missed her Walmart sweater that had been trashed in the fire. Shaun put his arm around her as they stood in line.

She ordered a latte and a scone for herself along with Karen's beloved banana bread. It felt perfectly natural for Shaun to have his arm encircling her waist—like they were "together," but something was off. Maybe it was the days of road grunge she was dealing with. After placing the order she took a detour by the bathroom to wash her face and give her hair a once-over. It wasn't much of an improvement but better than nothing.

When she came out of the ladies' room, Shaun was nowhere to be found. She assumed he was in the bathroom, as well. There was a barista-in-training behind the counter and a long line in front, so their coffee wasn't ready yet and she settled into a comfy chair. Five minutes later Shaun came in the front door with a plastic bag in hand. He sat across from her and slipped a gray Dallas Cowboys hoodie from the sack along with a new phone battery and charger combo.

"I bought it next door at Stop, Gas and Save. You were cold, and I owed you a battery," he explained, sliding the ever-present pocketknife from his jeans to cut the tiny plastic hook away from the sweatshirt jacket and slip it around her shoulders.

"They had phone batteries?"

"It's an urban truck stop. They have a little of everything."

"Thank you," she murmured, undone that he would have thought to buy her the hoodie.

"We'll get the battery charged up in the car. After you get Jason's file and key code turned over to the authorities, it won't matter what Donner taps into."

"How is he doing it?"

"I'm not sure but Zip Technologies has all kinds of experimental prototypes that were created in the development of Zip-Net. Illegal as hell to use outside the lab, but I doubt that's stopping Michael right now."

She nodded and he rested the back of his palm on her cheek, then her forehead. "Your asthma, it's getting worse isn't it?"

She shrugged. "I'll be okay once I'm out of the city." Of course, this was spring in Dallas with every pollen known to man plus some they'd never heard of—the worst place for allergies on earth.

"I think you're being overly optimistic," he replied, shaking his head and surprising her completely by leaning forward and kissing her so thoroughly she forgot they were in the middle of Starbucks.

He pulled away first and for a moment there was such

despair in his eyes. She couldn't understand why. Then the barista was calling their orders, and his eyes changed to a cool blue-green in the early morning light and she wondered if she'd imagined that sadness.

He came back with their coffee and pastries and kissed her again before sitting across from her in an overstuffed chair. He tasted like a double shot espresso and she stared at him as he settled into his seat. Had something changed? He was more deliberate in his attention, more demonstrative. More direct.

What was it? Were they both less tense now that they were so close to getting the file and key code? She had no idea.

Yet when he took her hand on the way to the car, she had the oddest sense—it was as if it were for the last time.

Chapter Twenty

Karen's rehab center was located near White Rock Lake, a few blocks from the Dallas Arboretum and its sixty-six acres of botanical gardens. Once out of the car, Abby looked across the shimmering water where a couple of sailboats were out along with a few kayaks. She shivered in the cool morning breeze despite her new hoodie.

Forest green awnings dotted windows on the tan brick building behind her. Balconies facing the lake were filled with plants and wind chimes. It was comforting to know that Karen had such lovely surroundings for her recovery.

Shaun slipped his jacket around her shoulders and took her hand, twining his fingers with hers as they crossed the parking lot and entered the rehab facility. When they found Karen's room, a nurse informed them that she was at physical therapy and should be back anytime.

A few minutes later Karen was rolled inside in a wheelchair and stretched out her arms for a hug. "Abby, honey, how are you? I'm so glad to finally see you. So sorry it's like this."

Abby nodded, pulling back and feeling the tears behind

her eyes. "I'm glad to see you, too. I'm better now that I'm here."

Shaun started backing out of the room. But Abby held out her hand and he took it again. "Wait." She pulled him to her side. "I want you to meet someone."

Karen's eyes twinkled. "So this is your Irishman."

Shaun took her offered palm. "'Tis a pleasure to meet you."

"Abby's told me just enough about you to make me very curious."

He smiled and Abby watched as he proceeded to charm her friend.

"You have the package from Jason?" Abby eventually prompted.

Karen handed over a FedEx envelope that had been opened. Inside was a manila envelope addressed to Abby. She ripped it open, as well. Inside were two flash drives and several sheets of paper filled with computer code.

"I have no idea what I'm looking at." She glanced back at Shaun.

He was inspecting the contents over her shoulder. "Me either, but we don't have to understand it." He scrutinized the top page. "These have to be the upgrade file and key code printed out. Is there anything else?"

She turned the packaging upside down. Another sealed envelope fell out. Her name was scrawled across the front in Jason's handwriting. She stared at it for a moment, felt those tears well again and knew she didn't want to open this in front of an audience.

"I'll be back in a bit," she said, stuffing the thumb drives in her hoodie pocket and carrying the printouts with her. She walked from the room down the hall to a small living area set up for the residents with a television and a telephone.

A half wall with a long row of potted plants on it formed a hidden corner that appeared to be for reading or just a little privacy from the general hustle and bustle. A small window provided a view across the parking lot to the Arboretum. There was an emergency exit door with a crash bar that she assumed led to stairs and a sign with a warning about an alarm sounding if the door opened. She took refuge there beneath the plants on a small sofa, out of sight to read her letter—tearing open the envelope and taking a deep breath, unsure of what she'd find.

Hey, Buttercup,

If you're reading this…I'm sorry. I assume I screwed up and I guess it was pretty bad. You must have gone on quite the treasure hunt to get this package. But I need you to do one more thing before we're done with all this.

Take these two thumb drives and the papers to Rob Kenny. He's an old friend from school who works for the FBI now and lives in Dallas. You met him once. Remember? His cell number is 555-759-5601.

If it's gone this far, he'll know what to do and how to contact the proper authorities. And, Abby, whatever you do, don't trust anyone with Zip Tech.

Whatever is going on, whatever happened to me, they're behind it.

God, it feels so melodramatic writing that. But if you're holding this letter, it means I wasn't there to retrieve the package from Karen—so it's true.

Damn, there is stuff I still want to do with my life. Things I wanted for both of us.

Be happy, Abby. Make every minute count. Thank

you for standing by me when Mother and Father wouldn't.

I love you, baby girl.
Jason

She swallowed hard. Breathing hurt. She struggled to hold the tears back but lost the battle as she closed the letter. At least in her corner no one could see her. Completely hidden with a box of tissue beside her from the end table, she let go and silently wept—closing out the sights and sounds of the world around her.

Long moments later, she sat with her head down—exhausted but better. The noises of the facility gradually seeped back into her consciousness. A television set was turned up a bit too loud in the rec room across the hallway. Nurses worked at their station a few feet away. The traffic bustled outside the window beside her.

Cutting through all that, she recognized the hushed tones of Shaun's lilting speech. Obviously he was on a phone call. She started to get up and go to him. She could use a strong shoulder right now, but something held her back.

What was it?

The tone of his voice?

The warning in Jason's letter?

Shaun was, after all, part of Zip Tech. But surely she could trust him? She'd trusted him enough to sleep with him.

"I said I'd do the job and fix things, Donner. I've done all you've asked and more. Every day we've talked. She trusts me. Why don't you?" His words faded as he walked toward the rec room.

Air tore at her throat as it left her lungs in a whoosh. She felt like she was going to be sick. She wanted to scream.

Shaun had talked to Donner every day?

Had everything been a lie?

How could she have been such a fool? She'd thought he felt something for her beyond obligation. But he'd only slept with her, lied to her, used her the whole time to get Jason's upgrades and key code.

The realization sank in as an elephant sat down on her chest. She reached for her rescue inhaler in a vain attempt to nudge the crushing weight off and took a quick hit of albuterol. It wasn't much use. Her lungs had been punished to the point of persecution over the past four days.

Damn it. She could not have another asthma attack.

She had to get out of here. Afterward, she could rage and die of humiliation, but right now there was no time. She had to leave before he saw her.

She looked around her little niche for a way to escape. The emergency exit was rigged with an alarm. Didn't matter. She had the thumb drives, the printouts and her brother's letter. She had to vanish. Now.

But Karen…

As if on cue, she spied a nurse wheeling her friend down the hall to what Abby assumed had to be another of her therapy appointments. Abby hunkered down farther to insure she couldn't be seen.

Karen was safe and Shaun was across the hall as he finished that phone call. She couldn't believe it had come to this. She tried to take another deep breath and felt the air ripping at her throat.

She wasn't going to be able to run away from him. She was going to have to "cab it." Or hide. Physically running was beyond her. It wasn't going to be feasible to even walk a long distance at anything more than a sedate pace.

She huddled in Shaun's jacket, alternately staring out the window at the gardens across the street and at the emergency exit door. Sliding her hands into the pockets of his Windbreaker, her fingers closed around…car keys?

Her heart leapt a little as she pulled them out to make sure that they were indeed the keys to Harlan's Jeep in the parking lot. Shaun had left them in his jacket, not thinking he'd be separated from her.

This was perfect. If she could just get to the vehicle, she'd be home free. She could lose herself in the city and call Jason's FBI friend to come get the upgrades and key code.

She pulled out her inhaler, took another puff and glanced over her shoulder. Shaun was still talking and standing in the doorway to the rec room.

She picked up Jason's papers and letter, quietly folding them, and put them in her jeans pocket alongside her albuterol. With one final exhalation through her nose she headed for the door—fearing that if she looked back, and met Shaun's piercing gaze, she'd turn to stone.

The screeching alarm shattered the quiet of the facility but she stayed calm.

Keep walking. Like you're supposed to be here. Don't panic.

If her luck held, everyone, including Shaun, would assume it was a resident making an unauthorized exit instead of her. But try as she might, she couldn't resist looking over her shoulder as she shut the door.

She didn't turn to stone. It might have been preferable. Instead, adrenaline coursed through her bloodstream when she made direct eye contact with him. Shaun's blue-green eyes were clouded by confusion then hardened into something dark and dangerous she hadn't seen directed at her before now. That "something" she hadn't wanted to believe he was really capable of.

Too late she realized her mistake. Her careful plan for

walking calmly down the stairs flew out the window. She saw a dead bolt toggle and locked it. Ignoring her tortured breathing and pinched lungs, she ran.

Chapter Twenty-One

Shaun broke off his argument with Donner in time to see Abigail slip through the emergency exit.

What the hell?

He ran for the door and made it just in time to hear a dead bolt lock into place.

Huh?

Then he realized. Hospitals and psych wards. Dead bolts were sometimes on the outer side of emergency exits for the patients with Alzheimer's.

The sign indicated another stairwell without an alarm by the elevators. He headed for it, knowing instantly why she'd run. She'd overheard him arguing with Donner.

He'd been getting calls throughout the night from his boss and he'd known he had to contact him. Convincing Donner that Shaun thought he still worked for him was necessary but only for a little longer. Shaun knew he should have gone downstairs to make the call, but he hadn't wanted to get too far away from Abigail or Karen.

What she'd heard sounded bad. Like he'd been working for Donner the whole time he'd been with her—driving her from Washington, helping her in Clarksdale, making love to her in the bed-and-breakfast in Alabama. Not telling her the truth had finally caught up to him.

He should have explained two days ago and certainly

yesterday. Now he had no idea if she'd even talk to him, but he had to try. Although first he had to catch her.

He found the stairs and was on the ground floor in less than sixty seconds. She couldn't be that far ahead. The woman was asthmatic and possibly running a fever, judging by the way she'd been shivering earlier.

He'd put his coat on her to—*shit*.

The Jeep keys were in his coat pocket. That was why she'd taken off like that. She'd known if she could just get to the car she'd be gone.

Damn it to hell.

He poured on the speed, bursting through the front doors in time to see her peeling out of the parking place. He sprinted across the asphalt, knowing it was too late but making a supreme effort anyway. He watched her fishtail out of the lot and into the traffic before barreling away. She didn't look back.

So this was the price he must pay for lying. Except he wasn't the one who would pay. Abigail would…with her life.

ABBY KEPT DRIVING EVEN AS she saw Shaun racing out of the entrance to the rehab center. She was coughing from her dash down the stairs—the constriction around her chest so tight she was becoming light-headed. If she could only get a few blocks away, she'd pull over and catch her breath. Then she'd be fine.

Rounding the corner, she saw a long ivy-covered fence topped every couple hundred feet by huge planters filled with blooming exotics. She peered through the leaves as she drove past a full parking lot. A massive sign stretched across the road announcing Dallas Blooms, the Dallas Arboretum's annual spring flower festival. A long line of cars headed inside. This appeared to be the perfect place to get lost for the afternoon and regain her strength.

Shaun would never guess she'd driven less than a mile away from the rehab center. Her other asthma meds were in the backseat. She could do a breathing treatment in a bathroom if she had to.

Stalled in slow-moving traffic, she was set to pull into the parking lot when her phone started ringing. Glancing at the caller ID, she was grateful that she'd plugged in her new battery to charge before they'd gone up to see Karen at the rehab center. She recognized Shaun's number from when he'd had her program it in earlier on their trek from D.C. He'd insisted in case they got separated. Well, this sure as hell counted as separation.

She took in as much air as she could and answered.

"Abigai—" he began.

She cut him off. "Why do you keep calling me that? Everyone calls me Abby."

Why that was the first thing that popped out when there were so many other pressing things to be asked, she had no idea.

"Never mind," she snapped. "Don't answer that. There's nothing you can say that will convince me that you're not scum."

"I understand you're angry. But what you overheard is not what it seems."

She coughed a sarcastic laugh. "Oh, really? So you haven't been in constant contact with Michael Donner the entire time we've been on our way here?"

"Yes, but it wasn't because I wanted to help him, you have to believe that. It was because I knew that if I said *no,* he'd just send someone else to follow you. Someone who would hurt you."

"I don't have to believe anything you say. But I am

curious. Is that why you had sex with me? To keep me compliant?" *My God, I was a fool.*

"No. I made love to you because I couldn't stop myself. I'm sorry I hurt you. I've never let myself get so involved with someone I was supposed to be protecting. I've never let them get this close. It's always been my unbreakable rule. Afterward, I couldn't tell you about Donner because I was afraid of this happening. I knew you'd leave and I couldn't let you go out on your own, unprotected. He'd have access to you then. You'd be vulnerable like you are now."

"Why didn't you say something back in D.C. or before we ever slept together?" she asked.

"Because I didn't know what you'd do. If Donner had thought I wasn't on board with the plan to keep in touch with him, he would have crushed us before we ever left town. He has those kinds of resources. I know I was wrong. I did it all wrong. But you have to believe this one thing. I never meant to hurt you." His Irish lilt was thicker over the phone—or it seemed that way when all she had to focus on was his voice.

"How can I believe anything else you ever tell me? You talked with him every day. You told him where we were. You told those men where we were going so they could burn my house down. You probably told them that we were going to Karen's to get the package and that I have it now."

"No, Abigail. No. I didn't."

"You told me that you were too broken to be fixed. That's the one thing you got right, Shaun." She knew she shouldn't be on the line any longer or the call could be traced. According to what Shaun said yesterday, Donner might even be recording her words. She snapped the phone shut before he could reply, slipping the cell into her bag as she pulled into the entrance for the gardens.

She needed a place to disappear for a while more than ever and the crowds were perfect cover.

She moved through the ticket line stopping only to ask about pay phones. The clerk behind the counter told her there was a phone bank at the concession stand in the middle of the property.

The warm spring day shone down on her as she walked with young parents, children and the elderly along the central walkway—the Paseo de Flores—then on through the main area of the gardens. Wiped out from her asthmatic sprint from the rehab facility, she wandered till she found a shady secluded corner to plop down in. She had to rest while she figured this out.

She used Shaun's waded up jacket and her new hoodie for a pillow and lay back on the grass. Slipping on sunglasses, she kept careful watch as she tried to wrap her mind around all she'd just learned.

Who could she turn to? She fingered Jason's letter and thought about the friend he'd mentioned. Could Rob Kenny be trusted? With Donner's capabilities it might be a risk to even use a pay phone, but this was her only option now. She'd take the chance.

Making her decision, she left her spot in the shade and walked toward the concession pavilion. The phone booths were around back and out in the sun. She pulled out her letter from Jason and dialed Rob's number. He picked up on the first ring.

"Rob, it's Abby Trevor, Jason's sister."

"Abby, of course. Great to hear from you. I haven't talked to Jason in a while. He left me a message last week and I haven't been able to catch up with him."

She pictured Rob with his all-American grin and blond-haired good looks. She'd had a terrible crush on him at one time. It was hard to believe he was an FBI agent now. And as much as she might desperately wish this was just a social hey-I'm-in-town-let's-get-together call, there was no way to beat around the bush.

"Jason died last week in a hit-and-run accident."

Rob gasped and started to give her condolences but she interrupted. "Only, it wasn't an accident. He was murdered. I have some information he left that he instructed be sent to you. When can we meet?"

It was so quiet that for a moment she thought the line had gone dead. "I'm very sorry for your loss. Jason was a good man."

"I appreciate that. Can you help me? I need to see you as soon as possible."

Her mother would have rolled in her grave at Abby's bluntness but Rob was unfazed. "Of course, I'll meet you," he said. "Where are you and what do you need?" All pretense of a casual conversation was over.

She wheezed a sigh of relief. "I'm at the Arboretum at White Rock Lake. How soon can you get here?"

"I'm in Arlington right now. With the traffic, it shouldn't take me more than about an hour or maybe a little over. Can you hang on till then?"

"I think so. I can hide if necessary," she said.

"Hopefully it won't come to that. But if you have to, hunker down and sit tight."

"All right, but you need to know there are people after me for this information. You could be in some danger, too, if you help."

"Don't worry about me, Abby. I can take care of myself. You just hold on."

Tears were threatening again. "Okay, I will. Thank you, I didn't know what else to do." She hung up and realized she wasn't getting much air. She'd been holding her breath on the phone. She leaned her head against the booth as dark spots danced in front of her eyes.

Crap. She pulled out the rescue inhaler and took another shot. The sun no longer felt pleasantly warm but hot. She needed something cool to drink. This was nerves most likely, but it didn't really matter. She could pass out just as easily from nerves as from a real asthma attack at this point.

She moved to the concession pavilion where it was marginally cooler. Taking slow breaths, she tried to calm her rising panic. Everything would be okay.

Rob would be here in an hour.

She could do anything for an hour.

Chapter Twenty-Two

Shaun paced in the lobby of the rehab center going slightly out of his mind. The situation was so much like Iraq he thought he was hallucinating—even down to the girl running away when he tried to explain he was helping her and her family get safely away from his boss.

Because Shaun had been on the phone with him when she ran, Donner knew Abigail was missing. To further enhance the nightmarish quality of the experience, Shaun had to act like none of this mattered when he talked to Donner a second time and heard the boss's plan. One of Zip Technologies's latest toys was just now up and running—privately and illegally tapping into the local phone lines and monitoring the airwaves for Abigail's voice using a brand-new protocol for voice recognition. If she used any phone in the area, the new program would find her, recording everything said by and to her.

Or Donner could also have her location as soon as Shaun called her back and talked long enough for a trace. With this new system, the process would only take about twenty seconds—a blindingly fast speed for a trace, much faster than anything developed to date. Thank God this new prototype hadn't been operational thirty minutes earlier when she'd hung up on Shaun. Donner would have had her location while Shaun would not.

There was no way around it. To save her, Shaun had to call her again and convince her to tell him where she was. But in calling her, he'd be betraying her at the same time because Donner would have the location, as well. And Shaun wasn't convinced Donner would tell him where she was if she wouldn't tell Shaun herself on the phone call.

Shaun had to convince Abigail he was telling the truth and then afterward he had to lie so well that Donner would be fooled. Lying would be so much easier, but if Abigail figured it out and bolted, she was dead. She could smell the lies on Shaun now, even over a cell connection.

But first he had to get her to pick up the phone.

Right…should be easy.

The desk clerk at the rehab let him use the office line to make the call since the clerk believed Shaun's phone to be out of battery power. Caller ID worked in his favor and Abigail picked up on the first ring. "Karen, are you okay?" she asked.

"Abigail, 'tis me. Don't hang up, Karen's fine. I used this phone so you'd answer. Please just listen."

He could only hear a slight wheezing and for the first time he was grateful for her asthma because he knew she was still on the line.

He took a deep breath and went for the whole truth.

"Donner can tap and trace calls…quite fast. He'll be able to get a trace on this call because he got your voice recorded when you used his phone in the hotel suite in D.C. And he has your cell number in the system now. He'll have people on their way to wherever you are. I can help. I can get to you first, but you've got to trust me."

Nothing but silence.

"Abigail?" He heard the strain in his own voice. He had to stay calm, but she had to talk to him and tell him where she was. Donner would have the information any second.

"Trust you?" She laughed bitterly. "Is this a new tack you're taking? Baffle the little woman with bull?"

"No, I…it's true."

"How can I possibly trust you? You've lied to me about everything."

He didn't know what to say. Donner had the trace by now but Shaun had no clue where she was. He could hear something in the background. Children squealing…a park maybe?

The truth was his only option.

"There's not a single reason I can think of as to why you should trust me. But I'm asking you to anyway," he said.

No sound. Then in the silence a faraway voice.

"Today at the Dallas Arboretum, we're proud to be hosting the North Texas winners of the Junior High National Strings Competition in a public concert. Join us on the concert lawn for the free performance starting in ten minutes."

She was at the Arboretum.

"I can help, Abigail. Please. Wait, don't hang up—"

The line went dead.

I can help.

Sure he could. Like he'd helped her right into bed and into this mess. Abby snapped her phone shut and stood.

How much of that announcement had he heard?

No way to know.

She should assume he'd heard it all and leave now. But where? Rob wasn't here yet. Should she wait on him?

Taking the car was no longer an option. If Donner's people had tapped any of her earlier calls, then they could already be on their way to the Arboretum looking for her.

It didn't matter anymore if she used her phone. Donner knew everything.

The only thing she could do was call Rob and warn him. She couldn't have him walking into this blind. She dialed his number but got voice mail.

"Rob, it's me. I'm still here but they know where I am. I'm in some trouble. I think they're tapping and tracing my calls. I can't say any more."

She headed back toward the *Paseo* intending to head to the parking lot but two men were on their way down the path hurrying along with the flow of concert traffic. They hadn't spotted her yet but one looked vaguely familiar.

Was that the man from her parents' house or was she imagining things? They'd gotten here so fast.

She took a hard left instead of going for the exit. She wasn't sure what she'd just seen but turning around to stare seemed a bad idea. Picking up her pace through the crowd that had suddenly grown rather dense, the constriction around her lungs grew tighter with each hurried step. The thought of Donner's men behind her had the elephant plunking its butt firmly down on her chest again.

"Join us on the concert lawn for the free performance starting in ten minutes." The recorded voice making the announcement had a clipped British accent, striking her as highly ironic given the circumstances and her location here in the heart of Texas.

She needed a place to hide till Rob came. She walked, studying the map given to her on the way in. A concert crowd could be the solution but she had no idea what kind of numbers were attending. Could she blend in?

The north side of the gardens appeared to have a sort of bamboo forest that wasn't even on the colorful graph of the grounds. That could be the ideal cover. She paused to casually sip from her water bottle and look over her shoulder.

The men were still behind her and the taller one was definitely the man from the fire. She was about to turn back to the path when she recognized another man talking on a phone behind the first two.

Michael Donner was here.

Blood rushed to her face. She froze and that's when they saw her. Tall Guy pointed and started for her. Donner's other man pulled a gun. She rushed along the path toward the bamboo forest, opposite the line of people headed for the concert.

Her breath was coming in wheezing gasps as dense stalks thirty and forty feet tall rose in front of her. The contrast was startling there on the edge of the well-groomed gardens and appeared to go on forever or at least to the edges of the property—like something you'd imagine on an Asian continent. She didn't hesitate or even glance over her shoulder, she just barreled off the sidewalk into the bamboo.

SHAUN'S CELL RANG AS SOON AS Abigail hung up. He knew who it was without looking at caller I.D. He was jogging toward the Arboretum but it was several blocks away.

"Sounds like you struck out, Logan." Donner's voice was cool, clinical.

"I had to go with the truth, Donner. She would have recognized anything less. You understand that. And it did the job of keeping her on the line. Did you get the location?" Shaun was at the curb waiting for a break in the traffic. The huge sign for Dallas Blooms was right above his head.

"Yeah, we got it."

Shaun stood perfectly still and took a calming breath.

He had to play this just right and sound calmer than he was. "So tell me where. I'll go, get the stuff and get out. Where is she exactly?"

He heard a low chuckle but it wasn't a pleasant sound. "I'm not sure you need to know. Hodges can handle things from here. I'll see you back in D.C. if you're so inclined to still work for me."

Damn. He tried counting to ten and made it to three.

"Christ, Michael, what's the deal? What do I have to do to prove myself to you?" His palms were slick on the phone. He had to get to the Arboretum now but it was a huge friggin' place. He needed to know where she was in there. He peered down the street waiting for the light to turn.

"Nothing, Shaun. That's the beautiful thing. Do nothing at all. Go home. Leave her be. Your work here's done. That's never been an issue for you before. Is it going to be now?"

Well, hell yes it was but he wasn't about to tell Donner that. Shaun forced himself to laugh. "Of course not. See you in D.C. I'll be driving back so it'll be a few days."

"No rush."

"Right. See you next week." Shaun shoved the phone in his pocket, saw a break in the traffic and ran.

STUMBLING INTO THE BAMBOO forest, Abby immediately felt cut off from the world even though she could still see the manicured grounds behind her. The men were racing along the path toward her—taking a shortcut across the lawn despite numerous plaques warning of dire consequences for those who walked on the grass.

She took one last look over her shoulder and started running herself. It was tough going through the heavy bamboo. Downed stalks blocked her path and darkness closed in for a moment before her eyes adjusted. Fallen branches caught in the oversized stems tore at her clothes and slapped at her face.

She pushed forward until she could no longer see the gardens behind her. Dried bamboo leaves crackled as she moved through the forest. She had to get to a hiding place and stop or they'd hear her.

How big was this thing? She stopped to get her bearings but it was difficult in the dim light. Only by looking straight up could she see the sun as it filtered through the branches and leaves. Her breathing was labored and her vision went dark around the edges. She sank to the ground with a plop.

Then she heard them, crashing through the brush somewhere off to the left and behind her.

"Hodges, where is she? You see her?"

"No. Split up. She can't go far. The woman's got asthma, for God's sake. There's no way she can run fast or go quietly."

The man called Hodges was right. They'd find her soon. Unfortunately she couldn't be completely quiet. Her breathing was going to give her away.

She dug her hand into the ground to get up and move forward. The sandy loam fell through her fingers and like that, she knew what she had to do.

She grabbed a small branch that had blown in from some other type of tree, got to her knees and began digging. It wouldn't have to be a deep hole but she needed a marker. Then she needed to move.

"Hodges, you in here?"

Her heart stuttered and her hands stilled as she recognized the Irish cadence in the words.

"Yeah, we're here. Where did you come from?" asked Hodges.

"Rehab center across the street," said Shaun. "Have you spoken to Donner?"

"Not since we got here. Thought you were on your way to D.C. Are you here to help?"

She held her breath. The moment of truth. Had everything Shaun told her been a lie?

He was within ten feet of her when he answered.

Shaun stepped into a slight clearing. "Sure, I just don't want to get shot at or blown up this time." There was a distinct edge to his voice.

"Sorry 'bout that." Hodges laughed but it had a rather nasty sound, indicating he wasn't very sorry at all. "How'd you know where we were?"

"Figured it out."

"Huh?"

"You leave a trail a blind man could follow in this bamboo."

The other, taller man barked a laugh.

"Screw you, Logan."

Shaun laughed. "Not that kind of guy, Hodges. Besides, security's on their way. You and your buddy there…chasing a woman across the Arboretum. Folks notice."

Hodges uttered a foul but creative string of expletives.

Abby clamped down on her lip till she tasted blood. Shaun had to know she was close by and listening to every word. Was he trying to tell her something? He'd asked her to trust him, but how could she?

"You've got to get out," urged Shaun. "I have a hard copy of everything Jason sent Karen Weathers. We don't need the sister. We don't have time to find her while she's hiding."

But Shaun didn't have the hard copy or the thumb drives. She had them. She'd specifically taken the printouts of the upgrade file and the key code with her into that waiting room to read Jason's letter. He knew that.

She wanted to assume he was lying to Hodges to protect her. The other option was too horrifying.

"This place will be crawling with security soon," said Shaun. "Maybe even cops."

"Feds or local?" asked Hodges.

"Does it matter? Get Donner and get out of here. He can't be part of this."

"What about the woman?" asked Hodges.

"Leave her to me," said Shaun.

Chapter Twenty-Three

Leave her to me.

What did that mean? Was Shaun going to kill her or save her? She hoped it was the latter and that she hadn't just made the biggest mistake of her life in the pick-a-good-man contest. Abby dug faster and as quietly as possible. She could still taste the blood where she'd practically bitten through her lip to keep from gasping when Shaun showed up and started talking. Sweat ran down the back of her ear as she pushed sandy dirt out of the hole.

Hodges sneered at Shaun. "You're the reason we're here now, Logan. You've screwed this up from the get-go."

"It was part of the cover. How was I supposed to get the information if I didn't go along with her? You wouldn't have gotten this far without me. Call Donner if you feel the need. But hurry. If cops get involved, you've got some explaining to do about the past week, don't you?"

"More than you know," murmured Tall Guy.

"Hodges, were you hiding in the cemetery?" asked Shaun.

She stopped digging to listen.

"Donner's orders." Hodges's tone made it clear he was proud to have been following them.

"You almost killed her. You almost killed me. I know Donner didn't tell you to do that," said Shaun.

She could hear the strain in his voice now. She'd noticed it over the past four days but hadn't recognized it for what it was till now. His accent thickened when he was stressed; the consonants were harder, the vowels softer.

"I was improvising. Besides, the bitch moved in time, didn't she? She's okay, so why are you whining?" Hodges was irritated and getting louder. Abby beat back the slick, oily coating of fear inside her belly.

"Well, hell, man, while I'm thankful for small favors, I'd appreciate it if you'd go to the practice range when we get home. I don't fancy having to hide whenever you strap on a gun. Now go fetch the boss."

She started digging again. The hole was almost big enough.

"Are you sure?" asked Hodges.

"Yes, I'm sure. I'll take care of her. Hodges, do you *want* to go to federal prison? There's no place to hide there."

Hide. Shaun had used that word multiple times. Message received. She prayed she was understanding him correctly and finished burying the flash drives and papers as the two men crashed away from her in the underbrush. That last comment about prison had gotten them moving.

A soft spring breeze stirred the bamboo but she didn't let the seemingly peaceful surroundings fool her. Shaun was here. Waiting to "take care of her."

She covered the hole and marked it with a small pile of branches before crawling silently away.

"Abigail darling, where are you? We've got to go now, before they find out I haven't spoken to Donner about anything we discussed here and come back."

Could she trust him?

Did she really have a choice? Of course she did. She huddled in the shadows, just out of sight and made her decision.

She knew this man. He was one of the good guys. He'd saved her on multiple occasions over the past four days. He was going to save her this time. She was betting her life on it.

"I'm here," she said softly, stepping into the dappled light.

HIS THROAT TIGHTENED AS SHE moved toward him. Her face was too pale and her lip was bleeding. There were scratches on her chin and her clothes were disheveled but she was alive. He intended to keep her that way. It was an effort to keep from reaching out to her.

"Did you hide the stuff?" he asked.

She nodded.

"Good. Don't tell me where."

He didn't want to know. Didn't want her to think he wanted the information. He'd let her tell the cops. He was out of this part of it.

He was watching her with all those thoughts running through his mind then she was in his arms. She was crying softly; he was kissing her hair and despite the danger, it just felt so right. She fit so right. He'd never thought he was going to hold her again.

He wanted to imagine for just a moment that she could be in his life for always. But he knew that was insanity. She'd never want him after all he'd put her through. Now was not the moment to be worrying about this—time was ticking away. He pulled back.

"Abigail, I'm sorry. I…I have a lot of things to answer for. I know that. But we've got to get out of here. Afterward, I'll tell you anything you want to know. Can you trust me till then?"

Her amber eyes were huge pools of fear and uncertainty. He couldn't blame her. He'd lied to her from the beginning.

But somewhere along the way, he'd stopped doing a job and started caring about her. Started dreaming of an impossible future with her.

Her lips turned up in a small smile. "Yes, I trust you."

He didn't deserve that but he was grateful. Pulling her closer, he kissed her softly before taking her hand. She was wheezing as he tugged her along through the bamboo and the undergrowth but he had no choice. They had to hurry.

Minutes later they were on the Paseo headed to the main gate with no crowds for cover. The first shot came from out of nowhere, going wide and striking a pot on the sidewalk beside them filled with ivy and flowing blossoms.

The clay container shattered into a million pieces, mixing with the dirt and flowers to litter the finely groomed grass and sidewalk like confetti. Shaun pushed Abigail ahead of him, shielding her as they ran. He could see the ticket kiosks up ahead but they were still thirty yards away.

Four more shots hit the sidewalk. Chips of concrete blew in the air, stinging his arms and face. They weren't going to make it. He pushed her toward a huge oak tree, just off the path. He was running behind her, making sure he was between her and the shooters. He was almost there and she was behind the tree when the sixth bullet hit its mark.

It was like being hit with a baseball bat.

He went down. Hard.

ABBY HEARD THE SICKENING sound of a bullet hitting flesh and turned from the cover of a massive oak to see Shaun fall and roll. He landed on his side just off the Paseo in a bed of white begonias.

He was conscious but unmoving. She reversed direction,

grabbed him under his armpits and pulled him behind the tree, blood oozing on the plants in their path.

"Are you okay?" That was a ridiculous question. Of course he wasn't. He was bleeding all over the white flowers they were sitting in, and trying to pull a gun from his shoulder holster at the same time. Then he was shoving the weapon into her hands. The hard steel felt cold and clinical here in the gardens. This was all happening too fast and she was wheezing like mad.

"Use this, now."

The gunmen were coming toward her. She could hear Hodges shouting directions to his partner.

"Oh, God," she murmured. "I don't know how. You... you're bleeding so much."

"Don't worry about that. Concentrate, Abigail. Look at me. I need you to focus on this." He pinned her with those remarkable blue-green eyes, filled now with pain and determination.

"The safety clicks off here." His fingers were shaking but he was showing her. She vaguely recalled hunting lessons with her dad from ages ago. She grabbed the gun, gripping it in both hands and stood—pointing it in front of her in a traditional shooter's pose.

Behind her she heard the *whop whop whop* of helicopter blades and sirens in the distance. The cavalry was coming. The only thing she didn't know was if the helicopter belonged to Donner or the authorities.

"Stop!" she shouted at the approaching gunmen. "Right there or I shoot."

"Abby." It was Donner, walking toward her emptyhanded as he continued to speak. "You don't want to do this."

"Oh, don't I?" She didn't have air to say much else.

The sirens were closer. She aimed and pulled the trigger. Dirt flew up at Donner's feet and he stopped walking.

"I don't have a gun, Abby. Would you shoot an unarmed man?"

"You really want me to answer that?" she wheezed.

"All right, we'll just stand here and talk for a moment. Where are the thumb drives?"

Maybe they'd go away if she told them the truth. "Don't...have them...anymore."

"What did you do with them?"

She listened to the sounds of the approaching helicopter. The police sirens were closer than she'd originally thought. Good thing. Her vision was getting spotty with the lack of oxygen. Adrenaline was the only thing keeping her upright.

"They're hidden. Can't get to them now and...you don't have time to make me before that...helicopter lands."

Shaun shouted over the cacophony. "'Tis over, Donner. You have to choose. Get out of here and maybe escape or stay and everything turns to dust. If you shoot us, who wins?"

"Shaun, I thought you knew me better. I always have a plan and I always win. If I can't have a happy ending, no one will." Donner shrugged. "It's my helicopter." He turned to Hodges who was still holding his gun on both of them and nodded.

Hodges smiled and raised his gun to take aim as another shot cracked across the garden. Blood bloomed on Hodges's white knit shirt and the gun fell from his hand. He looked down in surprise as a red stream poured from his left side and he crumpled like a pile of dirty laundry.

Abby looked over her shoulder to see blue-jacketed officers with FBI emblazoned across their chests running toward them. It registered with her that Rob Kenny really could take care of himself and he'd brought backup to prove it.

Donner raced for the helicopter landing on the lawn.

He was seconds from making it into the cockpit but the agents were faster and there were more of them. They surrounded the aircraft, pointing their weapons at the pilot.

Donner had lost.

Four agents were surrounding Abby, as well. She dropped the gun and sank to her knees beside Shaun. His eyes were open but his breathing sounded horribly labored.

"Please, he needs help," she gasped, her own airway quite compromised by now. She held her hands open so the agents could see that they were empty before pressing them against the wound. His blood pulsed warm against her fingers and even more of the flower blooms were stained red instead of white beneath him. She stared into his eyes, praying it wasn't for the last time.

"Don't you dare…leave me. You've got entirely too much explaining to do. Please, Shaun… Hang on." Her breath came in ragged gulps now.

The corners of his mouth turned up in the ghost of a smile but his eyelids fluttered closed as the agents surrounding them tried to take over.

One started to pull her away but another said, "Give her a moment. The EMTs are almost here."

"Shaun?" She grasped his hand and he squeezed it faintly. "Please…I need you. I'm here."

She was out of air as tears streamed down her face. She didn't want to move away but realized fighting with the agents would only interfere with getting Shaun the attention he needed.

"Ma'am, we'll take care of him," insisted the first agent. Then the EMTs were there and they were putting him on a gurney and she couldn't help it, she started to weep in earnest. Something inside her tore as they were wheeling Shaun away.

"Abby?" Another blue-coated agent came out of the crowd. It was Rob.

The tears came faster then and she couldn't breathe at all. He nodded sympathetically, patting her shoulder, mistaking her wheezing for tearful grieving.

"Please, Rob, let me…go with him, I…" She couldn't go on. Her own vision was going dark around the edges.

Rob nodded, not realizing the real physical distress she was in. "They're going to take care of him, Abby. I promise. And I'll take you to the hospital to be with him."

That would be good. She was going to need a hospital herself. That was her last lucid thought. Rob's voice was coming from a long way away. The elephant had moved from sitting on her chest to jumping up and down on it.

"Abby, are you all right?"

She nodded slowly but she wasn't sure what she was agreeing to anymore.

"Abby? What's wrong? Are you hit? Hey, someone get me an EMT."

If she could only exhale it would be okay but she couldn't because that damn elephant wouldn't budge. Rob was talking to her again but she couldn't understand a word. Then the ground was coming up to meet her and she knew nothing more.

Chapter Twenty-Four

Shaun lay in bed listening to the rain and watching the storm through the miniblinds. It was a half hour before he got more pain medication and he was counting the minutes.

He hurt.

Bad.

But he'd been damned lucky. If that ambulance hadn't been in route from another accident, he'd have bled to death, right there in the Arboretum. As it was, he was looking at a long recovery.

When he wasn't conscious he was dreaming wildly erotic dreams of Abigail or dark, violent ones of Donner, Hodges and Iraq—all thanks to his IV pain meds. He vacillated between not wanting to have them administered because he dreaded what they did to his head and craving the relief they offered.

Forty-eight hours since the shooting and he'd been conscious for a grand total of ten—all by himself except for the hospital staff and a visit from his friendly FBI agent, Rob Kenny. It had been a debriefing of sorts, bizarre and not a little awkward. Kenny obviously felt quite protective of Abigail and seemed determined to ascertain Shaun's intentions toward her.

Trouble was Shaun had no idea of his own intentions.

Before their tête-à-tête was over, Shaun had to wonder if Kenny was in love with Abigail himself. The idea of her being with someone like the blond-haired, blue-eyed FBI agent made him more than uncomfortable and irritable. He was just coherent enough to recognize his own jealousy.

Even after talking with Kenny, Shaun still had no idea where Abigail was. When he'd asked, the FBI agent had gone from friendly and forthcoming to hostile and tight-lipped, saying he wasn't at liberty to divulge any information. Official double-speak for I'm-not-going-to-tell-you-because-you're-the-last-one-who-needs-to-know.

Kenny was willing to share that Donner was in custody and the thumb drives had been recovered. The agent had called in backup after getting Abigail's second panicked call, hence the large number of both local and federal agents at the Arboretum. Since he was dealing with a Homeland Security issue, Shaun was surprised he'd been told that much.

The cable business channels were an even bigger source of information than the FBI on Michael Donner. The boss's arrest was huge news, even though Zip Technologies was a privately held company. Not surprisingly, the contract for Zip-Net to Homeland Security had been delayed indefinitely, but the venture capital investors and executive board for Zip Technologies had moved quickly to separate themselves from Donner and the scandal.

Being arrested by the FBI put you on a fast track out of the boardroom. Within twenty-four hours they had a new CEO and president. There was even talk of the start-up being acquired. Perhaps all those jobs at Zip Tech wouldn't be lost after all.

However on the subject of Abigail, Shaun was kept completely in the dark. Maybe she'd decided he really was too broken to deal with and was cutting her losses. He couldn't blame her.

But for as long as he lived, he'd remember her hanging on to his hand—begging him not to leave her there in the gardens in the Arboretum. She'd given him the will to hang on as he bled out all over those flowers. Or could that have just been one of his drug-induced hallucinations, too?

He'd lied to her so much. Surely she'd had enough and had taken herself back to England and her books. She was likely on a plane bound for London right now—to pick up the pieces of her life in academia.

He'd wanted it to be something different. Abigail was something he hadn't let himself hope for since…

Hope.

In a bed-and-breakfast in Alabama, she'd actually made him hope for the first time in so long.

How had he expected it to end? It didn't matter how good the sex was. She'd said from the beginning, *don't lie to me.*

So what had he done?

Lied to her at every turn, pretty much sabotaging everything from the very beginning before he'd even realized what she would come to mean to him.

Because it wasn't about sex. He was in love with her. And now he was alone.

Mother of God, when had this happened?

His shoulder throbbed mightily and he grimaced against the pain. What a time to figure things out. After the girl was gone and he couldn't go after her.

He squeezed the bridge of his nose in an attempt to stop his eyes from watering. Didn't work. He was going to lose it and cry, just like a preschooler, and it wasn't from the pain in his gut.

He glanced at the clock again, using words no three-year-old should know as the minute hand seemed to move backward.

There was a soft knock on the door.

Perfect, someone was here for his untouched dinner tray and about to see him in all his weeping glory.

"Come in," he murmured, wiping his eyes with the back of his hand.

Abigail stuck her head around the corner and his breath caught in his throat. He couldn't believe it. She carried a large bouquet of flowers but she was also wearing a hospital robe herself.

"Hey there," she said, shuffling into the room in hot pink leopard slippers. Her hair was piled on her head in a clip with a riot of curls around her too pale face. She looked amazing.

"I see you've been shopping without me." He found his voice but it cracked on the word *shopping*.

She smiled as she slid into the chair beside his bed, giving him a great view of her lovely legs and those sassy slippers. "Rob got them for me, to keep my feet warm on these linoleum floors. I had an asthma attack, a big one, in the gardens. They've just now taken me off oxygen."

He tried to ignore how the comment about Rob shopping for her slippers made him feel queasy and angry at the same time.

"Are you okay?" he asked.

"Yeah. They're discharging me tomorrow. Between all the smoke inhalation from the house and Jason's condo burning, plus running through the gardens and not taking my meds, I did a number on myself."

He nodded. "I'm sorry, Abigail. I didn't take very good care of you."

"What? Are you kidding? I'm not the one who got shot. How are you feeling?"

"I'm fine—" He stopped himself. "Actually, I hurt like hell. But I'm much better now that you're here. I appreciate your stopping by—"

He stopped talking. Her eyes glistened with unshed tears.

She stared at him a moment and finally said, "Rob explained a lot of things to me but I want…I need to know why. Why did Michael Donner do this? He had a product that was going to make him millions. Why did he kill my brother?"

"I don't know for certain. Greed? Ambition? There's always someone who wants more and there are so many out there who are willing to pay for information. For what it's worth, I don't think it was all about the money. I've known Michael Donner for two years and frankly, money isn't that big of a motivator for him."

Shaun shook his head and continued. "But power. Ah, now, that's huge. The man can't stand to lose at anything. With the spyware, he would have wielded remarkable influence. But he had to have the key code so he could sell that 'window into Homeland Security' to the highest bidder after the Zip-Net product was installed. Jason took that all away from him. And Donner didn't even realize it until after he'd had him killed."

She nodded, slowly absorbing all the information. "I don't know what I would have done if you hadn't been there."

He stared at the flowers she'd brought, unable to meet her eyes. "When I found out Donner knew your location there at the Arboretum, I was going crazy trying to find you."

"Thank you for everything. That sounds so inadequate. I wanted to visit earlier but the doctors wouldn't let me off my floor till today."

He broke his gaze from the flowers to glance at her. "No worries. You didn't have to come."

She cocked her head and looked at him strangely. "Well, you did save my life. Multiple times. It's the least I can do." She smiled as she said.that last part.

He didn't smile back. *Damn Rob Kenny, even if he was just explaining things.* Shaun stared, unable to look away. "I don't want you to feel obligated in any way, Abigail."

An awkward silence descended as a new nurse breezed in after a quick knock. "Oh, you have company. I'll be quick. I'm here with your pain medication."

"Can that wait?" he asked, hating the interruption and desperately needing a clear head for this conversation.

"No. You don't want to let that pain get ahead of you now, do you?" Before he could say he really didn't give a damn about that at the moment, she'd injected the narcotic into his IV.

He tried not to glare but he certainly did not want to have this discussion half-looped.

"Would you like me to put those flowers in water?" the nurse asked, unaware of what she'd done.

"Sure, thanks," muttered Shaun, suddenly utterly miserable. *Anything, but leave. Please.* The woman had just nuked his chances of having a coherent discussion with Abigail for the next six hours. She'd be long gone when he was lucid again.

The nurse took the bouquet, finally seeming to realize she was interfering with something important, and said nothing else other than a cheery, "Be back later."

Like I'll be awake then.

Abby stood and he thought she was leaving, too.

"Don't go," he said.

She sank to the edge of the bed, her expression inscrutable. "Shaun, I wasn't going anywhere and I need you to know I don't feel obligated to be here because you saved my life. I'm here because…I'm in love with you."

For a moment he thought he'd imagined her words. But it was too soon for the drugs to be kicking in. He gave a small shake of his head. "How is that possible?"

Her eyes widened. "So not the response I was hoping for." She stood up again.

"Wait." He reached for her hand, taking it firmly in his, hoping he made it through this conversation before the meds took effect. "I'm sorry. You really mess with my head and—"

Her expression grew cooler.

"God, I'm saying this all wrong. I've never felt like this, Abigail. I just figured it out before you walked in here. When I thought I'd lost you and the chance to tell you."

His eyes filled and he took her other hand. *Damn.* This was not how he wanted to tell her but she had to know, had to see what was really inside him with no walls. No more hiding behind that cool exterior he'd always shown to everyone when his emotions threatened to get in the way.

Taking a deep breath, he dove in. "I love you and I don't know how to go on without you. But after all I've put you through, I'm just wondering how you could feel the same way about me."

She laughed aloud, in genuine relief, and he felt…hope. It was still too fast for the meds to be making him feel woozy, so this sense of promise had to be real.

He raised an eyebrow. "I need you to explain. Really."

Her cheeks turned pink and he remembered meeting her for the first time—how lovely it had been seeing a woman who blushed.

She squeezed his hand. "For some reason I feel like I'm in fourth grade telling a boy I like him. I trust you and I never thought I'd say that. Your past doesn't scare me. You're a good man."

He didn't deserve this or her. "I'm not good. You don't really know me. You said it yourself. I'm too broken—"

She put a fingertip to his lips and smiled. "I was wrong to say that and I'm sorry. I don't know everything about you but I know enough. Enough to know I'm not looking for a way out or an escape hatch." She focused on his eyes. "Are you?"

He shook his head. This wasn't a dream. She wanted him. "You're it for me," he murmured.

She smiled and lifted her hand to wipe a tear from his cheek. "Then that's all there is. I love you, period. No conditions."

She was leaning toward him when he felt the first hazy bump of pain medication wash over him. Then she was kissing him and he felt her breath against his face but this was still real. He was done with trying to talk her out of it and he wasn't tempting fate anymore. Hadn't he given her fair warning? He no longer wanted to talk her out of anything, except maybe a few articles of her clothing.

She leaned in again, avoiding all the IV lines as he reached for her—touching her hair, longing to freeze this moment in time. He heard one of her slippers hit the floor.

"You really want this, don't you? You want me." He was caught in the wonder, even as his voice was slurring. The IV narcotic was definitely kicking in.

She grinned and nodded at the same. "Yes, I do. But I think I may have to tell you again when you wake up."

"Nope, I'll remember. I may even get to dream the good stuff now."

"What does that mean?"

"Tell you later. I'm knackered," he whispered, squeezing

her hand, knowing he was wearing a ridiculously goofy grin. His eyes drifted closed but he fought it hard. This was entirely too important.

"I'm all in, Abigail. I'm not letting you go…ever. Trust me."

"I do."

"And fifty years from now, you remember to tell our grandkids—I tried to warn you off but you wanted me anyway."

"I'll do that." She crossed her legs, a bare foot catching his eye before she kissed him again and his eyes drifted closed.

She'd be here when he woke up. He knew it with a certainty he hadn't felt in…never. Abigail would be here today, tomorrow and tomorrow. Life would never be the same.

* * * * *

COMING NEXT MONTH

Available May 10, 2011

#1275 BABY BOOTCAMP
Daddy Corps
Mallory Kane

#1276 BRANDED
Whitehorse, Montana: Chisholm Cattle Company
B.J. Daniels

#1277 DAMAGED
Colby Agency: The New Equalizers
Debra Webb

#1278 THE MAN FROM GOSSAMER RIDGE
Cooper Justice: Cold Case Investigation
Paula Graves

#1279 UNFORGETTABLE
Cassie Miles

#1280 BEAR CLAW CONSPIRACY
Bear Claw Creek Crime Lab
Jessica Andersen

REQUEST YOUR FREE BOOKS!
2 FREE NOVELS PLUS 2 FREE GIFTS!

Harlequin®

INTRIGUE®

BREATHTAKING ROMANTIC SUSPENSE

*With an evil force hell-bent on destruction,
two enemies must unite to find a truth that turns
all-too-personal when passions collide.*

*Enjoy a sneak peek in Jenna Kernan's next installment
in her original* TRACKER *series, GHOST STALKER,
available in May, only from Harlequin Nocturne.*

"**W**ho are you?" he snarled.

Jessie lifted her chin. "Your better."

His smile was cold. "Such arrogance could only come from a Niyanoka."

She nodded. "Why are you here?"

"I don't know." He glanced about her room. "I asked the birds to take me to a healer."

"And they have done so. Is that *all* you asked?"

"No. To lead them away from my friends." His eyes fluttered and she saw them roll over white.

Jessie straightened, preparing to flee, but he roused himself and mastered the momentary weakness. His eyes snapped open, locking on her.

Her heart hammered as she inched back.

"Lead who away?" she whispered, suddenly afraid of the answer.

"The ghosts. Nagi sent them to attack me so I would bring them to her."

The wolf must be deranged because Nagi did not send ghosts to attack living creatures. He captured the evil ones after their death if they refused to walk the Way of Souls, forcing them to face judgment.

"Her? The healer you seek is also female?"

"Michaela. She's Niyanoka, like you. The last Seer of Souls and Nagi wants her dead."

Jessie fell back to her seat on the carpet as the possibility of this ricocheted in her brain. Could it be true?

"Why should I believe you?" But she knew why. His black aura, the part that said he had been touched by death. Only a ghost could do that. But it made no sense.

Why would Nagi hunt one of her people and why would a Skinwalker want to protect her? She had been trained from birth to hate the Skinwalkers, to consider them a threat.

His intent blue eyes pinned her. Jessie felt her mouth go dry as she considered the impossible. Could the trickster be speaking the truth? Great Mystery, what evil was this?

She stared in astonishment. There was only one way to find her answers. But she had never even met a Skinwalker before and so did not even know if they dreamed.

But if he dreamed, she would have her chance to learn the truth.

Look for GHOST STALKER by Jenna Kernan,
available May only from Harlequin Nocturne,
wherever books and ebooks are sold.

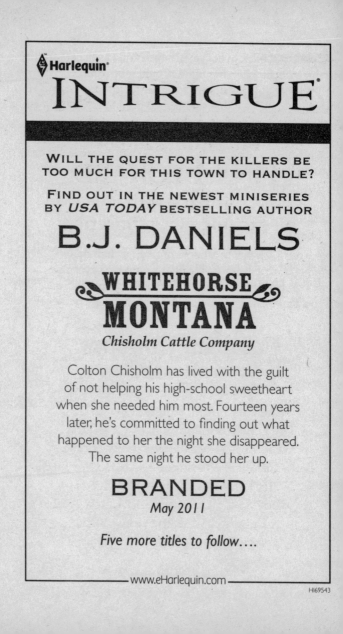